MIRANDA'S EXILE

Cate Murray

StoryAngles Publishing Co.

ISBN-13: 9798371635280
ISBN-10: B0BR8NHYQ2

Cover design by: C. L. Nichols

Printed in the United States of America

This story is dedicated to my ancestors who setttled in Bosque County after the Civil War.

CONTENTS

Title Page

Copyright

Dedication

Beaten and Banished 3

The New Piano Player 9

Drum Beats & Stew Meats 16

On a Mission 23

Ginger Ale 30

News from Home 37

A Courtly Invitation 44

Brothel Virgins 51

A Hen's Tail 58

Petrarch & Herrick 64

Across the Trinity 71

Texas Star 78

Civilized 84

Claddagh Lace 91

Letters from Ft. Worth 97

Soda Pop & Secrets 103

Arrangements 109

Goldilocks 115

Cotton Tulle 121
Hitch Up the Buggy 127
Bandits 133
A Rainy Rescue 141
Meridian 146
Apprehension 152
Guardian Angels 158
A Chance Meeting 164
4th of July 170
False Witness 177
Wedding Day 183
Awaiting a Child 189
Wedding Night 195
A Hot Kitchen 201
Birthday Surprises 207
Baby Bart 214
Disturbance in the Nursery 220
On the Road Again 226
Bartholomew Speaks 232
Asleep in the Manger 238
Search Party 244
God Bless Us 250
About The Author 259
Praise For Author 261
Books By This Author 263

A New Vella Story from Cate Murray
Miranda's Exile
Beaten & Banished
episode 1

BEATEN AND BANISHED

"I'll have no painted harlots in my family!" Abner Davis scrubbed the makeup off Miranda's face. "After I clean you up, you're packing up and leaving. No respectable farm girl needs four dresses!"

"She sewed them herself, Abner." Miranda's mother tried to defend her daughter. "Mrs. Wright gave her the material."

"Come with me, Mama!" Miranda pleaded.

"Mrs. Wright's a whore herself. Putting paint on my stepdaughter's face. Overpaying her for making dresses!"

"Mrs. Wright does not overpay Miranda. She sews beautifully," her mama said.

"Those bustles, and ruffles, and rickrack! Whore attire. From now on, this house is a godly house. Go pack your scandalous frocks." Abner slapped his stepdaughter across her face, landing her on the floor. He slapped her other side.

Miranda picked herself up, wiped her bloody nose with a rag, then went into her room and commenced packing.

"Hurry, so I can put you on the Fort Worth stagecoach." Abner gnarled. "You'll never spend another night here." Abner stalked outside to prepare the buggy.

Miranda and her stepfather said nothing during the bumpy buggy ride to Mrs. Wren's Stagecoach station. "Wait for us!" Abner yelled as the stagecoach passed them. Abner whipped the horses as he followed directly behind the coach. After a while, the driver blew his military horn to alert the people in Wren's Hotel.

"Here's enough to get her to Fort Worth," Abner told the driver as he handed him Miranda's bag. "But she's a whore. Dump her anywhere!"

Miranda entered the stagecoach, and a couple entered and sat across from her. "Good day," she said to her travel companions. They stared at her in silence. Miranda wanted to defend herself, but she realized the attempt would be useless. The coach pulled away, and Miranda looked at the post oaks and sheep outside the window. She pondered about where she would stay and how she would find work in Fort Worth. She had six dollars and eighty cents in her handbag. She wished she had placed the money in her corset because she had heard that Fort Worth are full of thieves.

"How old are you, girl?" the man sitting across from her finally spoke.

"Eighteen, Sir. My name is Miranda."

"Any education?"

"I graduated from the eighth grade, Sir." She wanted to tell him that she was the first in her class, and she had won district spelling bees and composition awards.

The man looked at her for a while, then he asked, "If you're an educated girl, why do you want to disgrace yourself?"

"I don't, Sir. My stepfather became angry because I had makeup on my face. He's a strict preacher. I'm not a harlot!" Miranda was finally able to defend herself.

The man didn't say anything else for hours. Miranda looked outside at the dust. Wildflowers were beginning to bloom on the hills. The couple continued to stare at her, but their countenance had softened.

The stagecoach made a short stop and the woman got out and bought some food. "Here," she said and handed Miranda a biscuit with meat inside.

"Thank you, Ma'am." Miranda was truly grateful as she had missed the midday meal earlier. When she finished, Miranda cleaned her face with a handkerchief. She noticed some blood on the cloth. The woman again said, "Here." She handed her a handkerchief with water on it. Miranda thanked her.

Before long, Miranda noticed shotgun houses being built on each side of the road. The man told his wife, "The railroad is building them for their workers. The Texas and Pacific will be rolling through Fort Worth soon. Out the east window, Miranda could see tracks being laid in the distance.

About half a mile later, the stagecoach stopped abruptly. The driver opened the door and told Miranda, "Here you go, young hussy! This is your stop." He threw her the bag.

"Wait a minute! This is not a stagecoach stop!" Miranda cried as the man rode whipped the horses forward.

"Excuse me, Ma'am," Miranda said to a woman in a plumed hat. "Is this Fort Worth?"

"This is Hell's Half Acre, Sugar. Need a job?"

Miranda's
Exile episode 2
The New Piano Player

THE NEW PIANO PLAYER

"I'm looking for work as a seamstress." Miranda brushed the hair from her eyes.

The plumed woman threw her head back and laughed heartily. "First, let's get out of the street. Some girls at my boardinghouse will probably give you some business. Men are always tearing their dresses. My name's Addie."

"I'm Miranda."

Addie led Miranda between a wagon storage and lines of shotgun houses to a larger house with daffodils and tulips planted in front. Two girls sat on the veranda.

"This here's Miranda. She says she's a seamstress." Addie motioned for the eighteen year old to come up the steps.

"Welcome to our cat house!" a girl with bad teeth said and pulled out a chair for the guest.

"Cat house?" Miranda put down her bag.

"House of ill repute," Addie said. "This girl is Esther, and this girl's named Carrie."

"Howdy-do," Carrie said. "There's cat houses all over Fort Worth, but ours the best and the friendliest!

"This may be a house of ill repute." Esther took a puff of her cigarette. "But it's in good repute with the law!"

"The police love us," Addie explained. "We entertain them for free. It beats crime and jail." She laughed and walked inside the house.

"Do you play the piano?" Carrie asked.

"Yes I do."

"Play for us." Carrie guided her inside.

Esther looked at Miranda's face. "Did your husband beat you up?"

"No, a preacher did." Miranda sat at the piano bench.

"That bastard!" Carrie put her hand on Miranda's shoulder.

"I agree." Miranda began playing "The Old Chisholm Trail," a tune she had heard from cowboys' harmonicas.

"Can you play something faster?" A woman with a foreign accent entered the parlor.

Miranda picked up the tempo of "The Old Chisholm Trail."

"Bravo! Bravo!" all of the women clapped.

"Play 'Jenny with the Light Brown Hair,' the woman with the foreign accent said.

Miranda played the Stephen Foster song.

When she finished, someone requested "Beautiful Dreamer," so Miranda played the other Foster composition.

"You can be our new piano player. I'm Madam Porter. I'm from Ireland. That's why I talk funny. It's called a brogue. Come with me."

"Your voice is beautiful," Miranda said.

"Sit here. If you find a brogue beautiful, you must be Irish. What is your name?"

"Miranda Carr, Ma'am."

"Carr. Irish. I thought so. Did you come here to play music?"

"Actually, I sought work as a seamstress. But I don't mind playing the piano." Miranda tried not to sound overeager or nervous.

"We can use both of those skills." Madam Porter looked into Miranda's eyes. "But do you mind making biscuits or doing laundry sometimes?"

“Oh, no. I helped my mother with cooking and housework.” The thought of her mother brought tears to her eyes.

Madam Porter looked at Miranda’s face. “Did I overhear that a preacher beat you?”

“Yes. My stepfather. I was punished for wearing makeup. He threw me out.”

Madam Porter nodded in sympathy. She swallowed then said, “You’ve never been with a man, have you?”

“No, Ma'am.”

“Some men request virgins and pay handsomely for them. But if you want to stay virtuous, that’s fine. I respect a girl’s choice, as long as she doesn’t judge the other girls.”

“I’m not judgmental. I’ve been unfairly judged myself.”

“If you wish to stay, you’ll get free board plus three meals per day. As for your other pay, there’ll be tips for piano playing, and a nickel a garment for mending."

"I can sew whole dresses, design bustles, crochet, and knit."

"I believe you, Honey," Madam Porter. "Your pay depends on our pay. With the railroad coming in a few months, we'll have more business. But right now commerce is rather dry."

Miranda couldn't believe her luck, so quickly after being expelled from home and coach. "Thank you so much, Ma'am. I promise to try my best."

Miranda's Exile
Episode 3
Drum Beats &
Stew Meats

DRUM BEATS & STEW MEATS

Miranda unpacked her bag and hung her wrinkled dresses into a wardrobe. “Where do you keep the iron?” she asked Carrie.

“Why don’t you wear one of my frocks for tonight,” Carrie said. “We wear about the same size.”

“Thank you so much.”

“Do you only have one corset?”

“Yes, it needs washing.”

“Wear one of mine. I did well one month and ordered three extras!”

“So you have four of them?” Miranda had

never heard of a woman owning more than two.

"Yeah, they're so hard to get dry. It's not always sunny outside."

"I'm so grateful, let me mend your garments free of charge."

"Here's some stockings. Now that we're sharing a room, I feel like we're sisters!"

"What's that wonderful smell?"

"We're having beef stew for supper. I don't know what spices Diana puts in it, but her stew is the best in the world."

"I haven't met Diana."

"She's our colored cook. She used to work for a cattleman, but he didn't treat her right. Madam Porter can't pay Diana as well as the cattleman did, but she treats her like a person. It's an unspoken rule around here that we treat Diana good."

"I believe that colored people are people. My stepfather believes they're from a cursed race. Sons of Ham or something. He's truly hateful."

Carrie looked at Miranda's face. "After seeing what he did to you, I especially believe so."

"Are there any other unspoken rules around here?" Miranda brushed her hair.

"Never take the Lord's name in vain. You can say hell or damn, but don't put God or Jesus in it."

"I believe in that."

Carrie continued, "Madam believes that magic of any kind is evil—card divination, crystal balls, seances. Madam Hart, at a house on Rusk Street, sometimes gives seances, and Madam Porter gets madder than a wet hen. She sprinkles holy water around this house whenever seances take place nigh!"

"Holy water?"

"Yes, Madam is Catholic. She sometimes attends mass at this couple's house. A church is being built on Throckmorton Street. She told us if she ever gets real sick, we are to run and get the priest."

Miranda winced at the irony. "She's strange, but I really like her."

"She saved your life, Miranda. Think about it. If you had to sleep on the streets, you'd be violated."

Miranda nodded. "She's like a guardian angel."

Miranda and Carrie heard drumbeats and the sounds of boys' voices.

Carrie turned toward the door. "The drumbeats are early tonight. Little boys are hired to advertise saloon shows. Usually when we hear the drums, it's time for supper. Let's finish dressing."

As soon as Miranda and Carrie were

dressed, they walked into the dining room. Carrie stood at her place, and Madam Porter instructed Miranda to sit beside her.

"Miranda, I want you to meet Diana. Diana, Miranda is our new piano player, dressmaker, and she can help you out whenever you are in a bind," Madam Porter said.

"Pleased to meet you." Miranda smiled.

"Blessings, Miranda." Diana placed a plate and bowl in front of Miranda. As soon as everyone had plates and bowls, a steaming pot of stew was placed on the table.

"Let's all bow our heads and ask the Lord for His many blessings," Madam Porter said. "In the holy name of Jesus, we thank you for our safety, for our daily bread, and for our fellowship. Protect our health and our well being, Amen."

As soon as Madam placed her napkin in her lap, and picked up her spoon, Miranda followed. "This is the best stew I've ever tasted," Miranda said.

"Someday I need to play Faro with Diana," Carrie said, "If I win, I get her family stew recipe." Everyone laughed except Esther who had been silent.

"Oh noooo! Damn, my tooth!" Esther cried.

"Miranda, quick!" Madam Porter stood. "Go to Lander's Saloon on Main Street and get Doc Holliday!"

Miranda's Exile
SALOON
Episode 4
On a Mission

ON A MISSION

Miranda ran as quickly as she could. Luckily she saw a sign that read Main Street.

"Not so fast, Pretty Girl!" a cowboy said.

"I'm looking for Lander's Saloon, Sir."

"I'll show you, but it's no place for a lady."

"I need to find Doc Holliday. Dental emergency."

Several men whistled as the cowboy led Miranda inside the dark saloon.

"Please," the cowboy pleaded. "She needs Doc Holliday. Dental crisis!"

"I'll operate on you, Sweetie!" a man pouring a shot joked.

"Doc's in this room back here," the bartender pointed. "Passed out earlier, but he might be coming around."

The cowboy knocked on the door. "Doc, Doc, it's an emergency!"

"What the hell!" a disheveled Doc Holliday answered the door.

"Sir, I'm sorry to bother you, Sir," Miranda said, "but my friend, Esther, has a terrific toothache. Please come!"

"Hon, I'm too drunk to help anyone right now. Where does Esther live?"

"She's at Madam Porter's house."

The cowboy stared at Miranda.

Doc scratched his head. "Go to the drugstore and get her some laudanum or some opium pills. Let her sleep it off, and I'll see her tomorrow. If you have some silver coins, tell a blacksmith to melt them down so I can make fillings."

"Thank you so much, Mr. Holliday."

Miranda left the saloon with the cowboy. "Take me to the drugstore."

"I will, but maybe we need to walk back inside and talk to the blacksmith. I have the coins." They turned back inside.

"Mr. Morris, this is Miranda. She's a friend of a girl who needs teeth fillings. Can you melt these two coins down, so Doc can fill her teeth with them?"

"I s'pose so. I'll melt them tomorrow morning, but Doc has to melt it some more to fit it right. First of all, where do I deliver it, and do I get paid for it?"

"The girl is at Madam Porter's, and here's your pay." The cowboy handed the blacksmith a dime and a nickel.

Once outside again, the cowboy said, "My name's Paul." He tipped his hat to Miranda.

"Thank you for helping me, Paul. Let me

repay you." They walked in the direction of the drugstore.

"Nah, you don't need to pay me back."

"Esther or Madam Porter will repay me. Three dollars is a bundle of money."

"In that case, you can repay me. But don't open your bag on the street. Here's the drugstore."

The door was locked, so Paul knocked.

"I'm already closed," a man said at the door.

"This young lady has a friend with a toothache. Doc Holliday can't attend to her until tomorrow. We need laudanum or something."

"I'm out of laudanum, but I have opium pills left."

"Opium pills, please." Miranda opened her handbag. She handed three silver dollars to Paul.

"Four for fifteen cents," the man said.

Miranda paid him, and he locked the door and turned off the lights.

"Let me walk you back," Paul told her. He took her arm.

"Thank you."

"How did you end up at Madam Porter's?"

"I play the piano, sew, and run errands only." She paused. "My stepfather threw me out of his house. He was mad because I had makeup on my face."

Paul saw the bruises on Miranda's gas-lit face. "He beat you before he turned you out, didn't he?"

Miranda nodded.

"My uncle beat me. That's why I left home. Pennsylvania. I was drafted into the Union Army. I'm afraid I'm a Yankee." He winked.

"That's fine. The war's been over for 11 years." Miranda started to say that her father died fighting for the Confederacy, but she decided to keep silent about it, at least for now.

"Where have you been all this time?" Madam opened the door for them.

"Doc is indisposed right now. He told me to get some opium pills for Esther. I also gave some coins to a blacksmith for Doc to make fillings."

"Thank you, Miranda. I should have known you were dependable. Esther has already taken some opium. Tomorrow, she'll probably need cocaine."

Miranda's Exile

Episode 5

Ginger Ale

GINGER ALE

Miranda stepped in with her new friend. "Madam, this young man is Paul." He stepped forward. "Paul, this is Madam Porter."

"Good to meet you." Paul said. "The girl with the toothache can have my cocaine. A partner gave me some when we rode out of Austin. I decided coffee was safer for staying awake." He handed the small bag to Madam.

Madam grinned widely as she took the bag. "Sit down, Paul. Miss Miranda will be playing the piano soon. Would you like a drink?"

"I'd like a temperance beverage if you have it."

"We have ginger ale. Miranda, go to the kitchen and fetch two ginger ales, one for you."

Miranda smiled at Madam and headed for

the kitchen.

"You missed your supper, Hon." Diana looked up from her knitting. All of the dishes were clean inside the cabinet.

"I bet your stew will be even better tomorrow morning. Where do you keep ginger ale?"

"Right down here. And in the back." Diana opened the bottom of a cabinet. She pulled two bottles of Verner's and handed them to Miranda. "They stay cooler if I keep them as far away from sunlight as possible."

"Thank you. They're cool enough for me."

"I better open them for you." Diana fetched the bottle opener.

"Do we serve the drinks directly from bottles here?"

"Please do. If you pour them in glasses, I have extra to wash."

Miranda reentered the parlor, and Madam Porter turned to leave the room. “If you two will excuse me. Nice to meet you, Paul.”

“Nice to meet you, too, Madam.”

Miranda handed Paul one of the bottles of ginger ale.

“Gracias, Senorita.” Paul accepted the bottle from her. “I picked up some Spanish from Mexican cowboys.”

“‘De nada.’ I studied it in the eighth grade.”

They sipped their drinks. Miranda struggled to make conversation. For the first time, she noticed that the room was painted mauve and a print of Blarney Castle hung next to the piano. Abner had not allowed her to court anyone, so talking with the opposite sex was a new enterprise.

A man in a top hat opened the door, and Addie walked in with him. Paul stood up and greeted the couple.

“Paul, this is Addie. Addie, this is Paul.”

“And this here’s Horace, Miranda and Paul.” Addie’s voice slurred. She had apparently consumed a few drinks. “He beat Doc Holliday in faro this morning!”

“Howdy!” Horace handed his top hat to Addie. She hung it on the hat rack next to Paul’s cowboy hat. “You must be the pretty little piano girl. Play ‘Dixie.’”

Miranda put down her drink and sat at the bench. She hit a few chords to determine the right key, then proceeded to play the Southern paean. At the end of the song, she received enthusiastic claps.

“Excellent!” Horace placed a gold coin in the small tray on the piano. “A girl who plays ‘Dixie’ that good deserves the best.

“Sir, I’m honored. But isn’t this a bit much?” Miranda picked up the coin. It was inscribed *Confederate States of America.*

"Didn't I say you deserved the best. Isn't that what your daddy told you?" Horace smelled like whisky.

"He told me he loved how the sunlight lit my hair. He died at Gettysburg." Thoughts of her father choked Miranda.

"So sorry, Honey." Horace looked down. "Was he fighting for the Confederacy?"

"Yes, Sir."

Paul smiled at her.

"Then here's another!" Horace placed another gold in the tip tray. "A gold coin for a golden girl."

"Thank you. Let me earn it by playing some more for you. What else would you like to hear?"

As soon as Horace opened his mouth for the next request, Esther burst into the room. Her hair looked like a giant bird's nest, and she was wearing a nightgown. "Did I hear something about a gold coin?" she drawled. "I need it melted down for my fillings tomorrow!"

Madam Porter had heard and re-entered the room. "You go right back to bed, Miss Esther! Those coins belong to Miss Miranda."

News from Home
In 1876, Miranda's stepfather beats her and throws her out of her home. Her crime is wearing makeup. She travels by stagecoach to Fort Worth, Texas hoping to support herself as a seamstress, but is let off by the driver in Hell's Half Acre, the infamous gambling and red-light district. She encounters shady characters who attempt to entice her into a less honest trade. Miranda, though, is determined to survive respectfully.
Miranda's Exile
Episode 6
Cate Murray

NEWS FROM HOME

Miranda slept later than she ever had the next day. The sun shone brightly through the curtains. She heard moans coming from the direction of Esther's room.

"This one is rotten," a voice that sounded like Doc Holliday said. "I'll have to pull it. But it looks like I can cover the others."

Miranda answered a knock at the door. The blacksmith, Mr. Morris, held some shapeless metal. "Hello, young lady. I melted down those coins, but I need to talk with Doc."

"Come this way." Miranda led him into Esther's room. Esther's head lay cushioned in numerous towels.

"Hello, Doc," Mr. Morris said, "I liquefied two silver dollars for the girl's teeth, but I don't know how to shape them."

"I'll make a beeswax impression of her two front teeth and have Miss Miranda deliver it to you. It won't take long."

The blacksmith left for his smithery, and Miranda fetched a candle from Esther's dresser.

"Soften the wax in hot water," Doc told her. He took a folded bandanna from his pocket and unfolded it, then made a triangle out of it and tied it around his nose and mouth. Esther screamed, and Madam ran into the room.

"Esther, you hush! He's your dentist; he's not a bandit!"

Miranda walked into the kitchen and put some water on for boiling. Diana walked in, and Miranda told her the purpose of boiling the water.

"I'll melt part of the candle for you," Diana said. "Come back in a few minutes.

Miranda returned to Esther's bedroom.

"Miss Mary," Doc said to Madam, "Looks

like I can save most of Esther's teeth. I'll pull the rotten molar and cover the front incisors."

"Thank you, Doctor Holliday. When the ordeal is over, write me up a bill, and I'll pay."

"I'll service you for a reasonable rate," Doc told Madam.

"When you gonna pull the tooth?" Esther mumbled.

Doc stroked her hair. "I'll make the beeswax impression first. There might be too much blood otherwise."

A few minutes later, Doc Holliday turned to Miranda. "The beeswax should be soft enough now."

She returned to the kitchen, received the small tray of wax from Diana, and brought it to Doc. He pinched some of the wax. "Open up, Esther. There. Keep your mouth open. Don't close for a few minutes. I'm making an impression of your teeth. I'm putting my finger in your mouth. Don't bite it!"

After a few minutes, Doc told Miranda,

"Find a box to carry the impression in." She turned and saw Addie standing at the door.

"I'll get my hatbox. It's big, but the impression will be safe in there." Addie left the room. She returned and handed Miranda the hatbox, instructing her to hold the box upright.

"Where's Mr. Morris's smithery?" she asked Addie.

"On Main Street a block from Lander's Saloon."

Miranda found Mr. Morris attempting to shoe an ornery horse. Miranda stood away, and Paul came from behind her.

"How are you today?"

"Fine. I'm holding a delicate impression of Esther's teeth for Mr. Morris to mold the silver."

"Good," Paul said, "I'll help him with the horse. Paul gently walked up to the mare and took hold of the bridle. "Calm down, Girl. That's good. Easy now. I wish I had some sugar to give her."

"Then Doc would have to fix the mare's teeth!" Mr. Morris joked. They all laughed.

"Paul, you certainly know horses," Miranda said. "Everyone has them but few understand them."

"He's almost a hypnotist with them," Mr. Morris said.

"No, I just love them. In the war, I saw too many of them shot." Soon the mare was shod and placed into a stall.

Mr. Morris washed his hands and looked at the beeswax impression. "I s'pose I can use the impression to make silver covers for her teeth. It'll take awhile. I'll let Paul deliver it when it's ready."

"I'll walk you home." Paul took Miranda's arm.

As they walked down Main Street, Paul greeted a tall man wearing a badge. "Hello Mr.

Courtright."

"Hello, Paul," the man with the badge said.

Courtright looked at Miranda. "You're new in town. Are you Miss Miranda Carr?

"Yes, Sir."

Mr. Courtright took off his hat. "Miss Carr, I hate to inform you, but your stepfather has been killed."

Episode 7
Miranda's Exile
A Courtly
Invitation
Cate Murray

A COURTLY INVITATION

Miranda felt uneasy on her feet. Paul held her up. "What happened?" she asked Courtright.

"Let's step into my office here. The "office" was Lander's Saloon. Courtright looked at Paul, then at Miranda. "Are you also a teetotaler?"

"Yes Sir."

Courtright ordered sarsaparillas for Miranda and Paul and a beer for himself. While they waited for the drinks, the city Marshall pulled a telegram from his pocket and unfolded it. "This telegram is addressed to you, Miranda. The address is "General Delivery." He handed the paper to her.

It read, *Abner died in shame. His brother has farm. Leaving for Dallas. Love, Mama*

"Rather long for a telegram," Courtright said, "But I assume your mama needed to communicate quite a bit to you. The shame she wrote about means Abner was caught with another man's wife. The husband found him and shot both of them. Perfectly legal. I checked with Johnson County to be sure. They telegraphed back. It will be in the papers tomorrow."

"Hypocrite! He was a preacher." Miranda said. "I feel bad for Mama, though. She loved the son of a bitch." Miranda had never said an expletive before, so she winced.

"Abner beat Miranda for wearing makeup and turned her out of his home." Paul explained. Courtright looked at Miranda's face.

Courtright put his hat back on. "I'm sorry for what he did to you, but you won't have to worry about Abner any more." He gulped down his beer. "If I need to find you again, where are you staying?"

"Mrs. Porter's boardinghouse. I play the piano."

Courtright smiled. "You two enjoy your sarsaparillas. I have some more business to attend to."

Courtright left, and Paul glanced at the kitchen clock behind the bar. "Guess we need to check to see if Mr. Morris is finished with the silver teeth covering." They finished their sarsaparillas and stepped onto the boardwalk.

Paul took Miranda's arm and held the hatbox in the other. "Does your mama have relatives in Dallas?"

"My married sister lives there. Her husband is in the lumber business, so hopefully they can take her in and help her."

"Since the railroad came in, Dallas has been booming. Fort Worth will be a boomtown in a few months." Paul escorted Miranda away from the dog sleeping in front of the drugstore steps.

Mr. Morris greeted Miranda. "Hope it fits. I heard that Doc has some special glue. He can do things that other dentists can't." The blacksmith placed his creation in the hatbox and handed the box to Paul. Miranda and Paul headed in the direction of the boardinghouse.

"So did you and your mother come to Texas from elsewhere?" Paul asked.

"Yes, I was born in Marion County, Alabama. My papa was in an Alabama regiment during the war."

"So he wasn't in the Texas Brigade?"

"No. After the war ended, Mama decided to join a wagon train traveling to Texas. We lived on nothing but beans and biscuits on the long trip. Three months just to reach Texas. Other families in the wagon train took cattle and sheep. I had to help herd them."

"Sounds like you were on a major trail drive." Paul smiled. "That's what I've done since the war ended. Business slowed beginning with the Panic of 1873, but it picks up from time to time. When the railroad comes, the cattle industry will really take off."

"So you've been across the Red River to

Indian Territory and beyond!"

"Yes, Ma'am. Some of the best friends I have are Cherokee scouts."

"I would love to travel some day," Miranda said. "Except for the trail drive, as you put it, I've barely traveled."

"How about traveling with me, in a rented carriage, to the home of Mrs. Jacob Samuels? She giving a ball two weeks from now."

He wants to court me? Of course he does, Miranda thought. "I would love to. Forgive me if I seem nervous. Strange things have happened today."

"I agree. News of your stepfather and an invitation to a ball. The Samuels are Jewish. Do you accept people of the Jewish persuasion?"

"I've never known any. But I honor them as people of the Bible."

"Miranda, I have something else to ask you before we cross the street." Paul looked into her eyes. “Will you be my girl?”

Brothel Virgins

In 1876, Miranda's stepfather beats her and throws her out of her home. Her crime is wearing makeup. She travels by stagecoach to Fort Worth, Texas hoping to support herself as a seamstress, but is let off by the driver in Hell's Half Acre, the infamous gambling and red-light district. She encounters shady characters who attempt to entice her into a less honest trade. Miranda, though, is determined to survive respectfully.

Miranda's Exile

Episode 8

Cate Murray

BROTHEL VIRGINS

Doc Holliday looked up from the newspaper he was reading. "Did y'all get married while you were out?"

Miranda blushed.

"Jim Courtright just told Miranda her stepfather has been killed," Paul said.

"Good riddance!" Cassie said. "He beat her up and turned her out."

"I feel sorry for Mama." Miranda took off her hat. "He didn't even leave her the farm. She's going to Dallas to stay with my sister."

Doc pointed to a news story. "Was your stepfather a preacher who lived in Johnson County?"

Miranda looked at the print. "Yes, the

story's about him, Abner Davis. He judged everyone else while he was the most guilty."

Doc folded up the newspaper. "Still, his death must be a shock to you."

"Yes, Sir."

Paul placed the hatbox down on the table and opened it. "Hopefully, you can fit this silver on Esther's teeth."

Doc held the silver mold and turned it around. "Looks good. I'll try to fit it on her before she falls asleep. The two drugs she's taken work against each other. I'm going to need two pencils to keep her mouth open."

"I know where Madam keeps the pencils. Let me assist you now." Cassie left the room.

"Miss Mary," Doc called out, "I'm going to need a drink after I fit the girl's teeth."

Madam Porter stepped into the room. "You may have a bottle of my best rotgut. After the railroad arrives, I'll be ordering some good Irish whiskey, and we'll drink a toast!"

"I can't wait, Miss Mary, but today I'll take any whiskey I can get!" Doc laughed. He picks up the silver mold. Cassie handed him the pencils. "Miss Mary, I may need the assistance from both you and Miss Cassie."

"Do you need my help?" Miranda stood up.

"No, you stay in the parlor with Paul." Madam winked.

Miranda looked shyly at her beau. "Guess I better return the hatbox to Addie."

"Wait a few seconds," Paul said. "Is the answer yes or no?"

"Yes, I'd be proud to be your girl."

"Kiss me, then." They kissed and Addie walked in. She smiled.

"I assume that kissing is allowed in this house," Paul joked.

"Kissing, petting, and riding as well!" Addie laughed.

"Thank you so much for letting us borrow the hatbox." Miranda handed the box to Addie.

"I get the message!" Addie winked as she left the parlor.

Miranda sat next to Paul, and he placed his arm around her. "Would you like to hear about my life?" he asked.

"Certainly."

"I told you that after the war I rode on trails. The pay isn't much, but I managed to save most of what I earned over ten years. My aim is to own a ranch someday, maybe in Bosque County. It's beautiful land with rolling hills and many trees. Cattle need trees to stay cooler in the summertime."

"Where is Bosque County?"

"About 60 miles south of here. The land

isn't perfect for grazing, but it's good enough and cheaper than more perfect land. I used to ride through there with the Chisholm "

"Are you working at all while you wait for the next trail ride?" Miranda hoped she didn't sound judgmental.

"I get room and board at the Transcontinental Hotel for running errands and doing odd jobs. It's about two and a half miles from here. But until the railroad rolls through, there's less odd jobs. But, again, I saved most of my money."

"You don't drink, and I assume you don't gamble," Miranda said.

"I don't drink, gamble, or fornicate." He looked at his girl. "I never have, anyway."

Then that makes us both virgins, Miranda thought.

Cassie ran into the parlor. "Quick! Get a doctor, something's wrong with Esther!"

“I’ll go alone,” Paul said, “So I can run faster.”

A Hen's Tail

In 1876, Miranda's stepfather beats her and throws her out of her home. Her crime is wearing makeup. She travels by stagecoach to Fort Worth, Texas hoping to support herself as a seamstress, but is let off by the driver in Hell's Half Acre, the infamous gambling and red-light district. She encounters shady characters who attempt to entice her into a less honest trade. Miranda, though, is determined to survive respectfully.

Miranda's Exile

Episode 9

Murray

A HEN'S TAIL

The whole house gathered around Esther's bed. Esther's hand was on her chest. She moaned.

Doc held her other hand and took her pulse. "It's her heart," he said. "I wanted her out of pain, but cocaine on top of opium pills wasn't a good idea."

Diana looked at Doc. "I'm growing foxglove in my herb garden. Mr. Jones at the feed store said it is good for heart trouble."

"Very good," Doc answered. "But be careful. Crush one half of a leaf, prepare a tea, and strain it carefully. And wash your own hands before and after. Foxglove, in large amounts, is dangerous."

"Right away, Dr. Holliday." Diana left the room.

Esther opened her mouth to say something. Miranda saw her new silver teeth. "My chest and neck hurt."

"Try to rest, Esther dear," Madam said, "Diana's making you some tea that will help you feel better. And Dr. MacDonald is on the way."

"Is there anything I can do, Doc?" Miranda asked.

Doc touched Esther's forehead. "If her fever rises, we may have to put her in a tub of cool water. I hope your beau gets here with Dr. Mac soon. Right now, there's not much any of us can do."

Madam looked at Miranda. "You're a godsend, Dear. It would help all of us if you'd play a happy but calm tune on the piano. Leave the door open, so Esther can hear."

"Yes, Ma'am." Miranda left for the parlor, sat down, and played "Molly Malone." It was another song she had heard cowboys play on harmonicas. After a minute, Miranda heard a beautiful soprano. Madam sang the words. Miranda had never before heard the words: "*In fair Dublin city / Where the girls are so pretty / I first set my eyes on sweet Molly Malone...*"

Miranda continued playing. As she heard the verses where Molly dies of a fever, she decides to play another tune next. Paul walked in with Dr. MacDonald.

"Beautiful." Paul sat in the parlor. "Can you play, 'Gay as a Lark'?"

"Can you hum it for me?" she asked.

"Here," Paul said and pulled out a harmonica. He began playing. After awhile, Miranda joined him in a duet.

"You seem to know more about treating a mild heart attack than I do!" Miranda overheard a male voice say. He walked through the parlor carrying his black bag. "Filthy whores!" he muttered as Paul held the door for him.

Tears formed in Miranda's eyes. "Why does Dr. MacDonald judge so cruelly?"

"There's a double standard that I've never understood," Paul said. "The same action that supposedly makes a boy a man, makes a girl a whore. I try to respect women instead of using them." He paused, then said, "Sometimes unfortunate events propel women toward a life that they otherwise would not have chosen."

Miranda played "Fur Elise." As she completed the last notes, Cassie walked in and clapped. "Esther wants you to play, 'Jesus, Savior, Pilot Me.'"

"Certainly." Hymns made Miranda uneasy although she believed in Jesus. Hymns brought back bad memories of playing for Abner's church. For Esther's sake, though, she played. When she finished, she noticed she had a large audience in the parlor. She asked Doc, "How's Esther?"

"The patient is ready for a dance. The dentist needs a cocktail or a hen's tail or something strong."

"I'll bring you the best we have, Dr. Holliday." Diana left for the kitchen.

A knock was heard at the door. Paul opened the door, and a well-dressed man stood in the doorway and spoke, “I’m looking for Miss Miranda Carr.”

Miranda stood up at the piano bench. “Yes, Sir.”

“Miss Carr, I’m a Pinkerton detective...”

Petrarch & Herrick
Miranda's
Exile
Cate Murray

PETRARCH & HERRICK

"My name is Mr. Chadwick," the Pinkerton detective said. "May I come in?"

"Yes, you may sit down," Madam Porter showed Chadwick to a chair.

The detective looked at Miranda. "Do you work here?"

"Yes, I play the piano and run errands."

"If the picture I have of you is a good likeness, you are Miranda Carr."

"Yes, Sir."

"Your sister, Mrs. Graham, hired me to find you. She feared you would be in this part of

Fort Worth."

Miranda held up her head. "You may tell Clotilda that I am treated very well here."

Mr. Chadwick looked around the parlor. "Mrs. Graham wants you to travel back to Dallas with me. She wants you to stay with her along with your mother."

"I knew mama is now in Dallas with Clotilda, but I'm fine here. I will write her." Miranda held hands with Paul.

"Why don't you go for a visit, Miranda?" Madam said. "Business will remain slow around here until the train rolls through. Your mother needs conforting."

Miranda looked at Madam's eyes, then she looked at Paul.

Paul finally spoke. "Family is important. I was three when I lost my mother. I never knew my father. I will wait for you."

Mr. Chadwick spoke next. "If you come with me, we can catch the 7:00 morning stagecoach to Eagle Ford. From there, we'll ride the train into Dallas. We'll take a long trip and a short trip."

"How far is it to Eagle Ford?" Miranda asked.

"Twenty-one miles," Chadwick answered. "About 10 miles less than from Cleburne to Fort Worth."

Miranda looked at Mr. Chadwick. "I'll go. Do I meet you somewhere tomorrow morning?"

"No, I'll pick you up here at 6:15. We'll catch the coach at the Transcontinental Hotel."

"And I'll tell Diana to boil you some eggs for the trip." Madam put her arms around Miranda.

"Then I will see you at 6:15 tomorrow." Mr. Chadwick put on his hat and left.

Madam hugged Paul. "I want you to stay for supper. Chicken and dumplings. You've helped us so much around here."

"Thank you, I'm glad to help. I'll be glad to have supper with you. Is there anything I can do for you now?"

"The rest of us will leave this parlor, and you and Miranda can catch up on what you need to catch up on. You won't see each other for a couple of weeks, so we need to leave you two alone." Madam and the others left the room.

Miranda turned to Paul. "I really don't want to go to Dallas. My sister always bullied me."

"People sometimes change. Give her a chance."

Miranda sighed. "I'll try. It was probably Mama's idea to find me."

"Yes, your mother had been widowed twice."

"My father was her great love. Let's change the subject. Away from the dead. If I seem awkward, remember that I've never had a beau before."

"You can be gawky around me. I might be accidentally gawky too."

"You have beautiful brown eyes, Paul."

"And Miranda, your gray eyes are like stars, truly. You have a Shakespearean name, and Shakespeare was anti-Petrarchan, but here I am describing you with a petrarchan image."

Miranda blushed. "I love Renaissance poetry—Petrarch, Shakespeare, but especially Robert Herrick."

"He's my favorite too," Paul said. "I used to read a thick book of poetry on trail rides. The cook let me put the book in the chuck wagon because it was too big to carry with me."

"What are your favorite lines?"

"I love all the anti-puritan poems, "Miranda said, "especially those of the beauty of nature: *'I sing of brooks, of bowers, / of April, May, of June, and July flowers.'*"

Paul pauses and Miranda proceeds, *"I sing of Maypoles, hock carts, wassails, wakes, / Of bridegrooms, brides, and their wedding cakes…"*

She paused and Paul looked at her. "Miranda, I love you. Will you marry me?"

Across the Trinity
Miranda's Exile
episode 11
Cate Murray

ACROSS THE TRINITY

When Miranda and Paul kissed good night, he promised he would wait for her answer. *Should I marry Paul? I haven't known him long, but I love him. Would I be happy in a limestone house in Bosque County? Are these doubts the result of Abner's treatment of Mama and me? Abner was quite the charmer until he put the ring on Mama's finger. No, Paul's not Abner; he's real. Did God choose him for me?*

Paul met Miranda in front of the Transcontinental Hotel, and he waited with her under a great oak tree.

"Yes," she whispered to her beau as he helped her step off Chadwick's rented buggy.

Paul smiled at her to show her he heard. Since there were other people around, he spoke of things rather than marriage. "This is the site of the actual military fort – Fort Worth. Back in 1849, settlers had trouble with the Comanches, so the military moved in and built buildings and fences. As you can see, the original fort is gone now."

Miranda changed the subject. "When are you leaving for your trail drive?"

"Tuesday. It'll probably be my last trail drive. The railroad will come in and change how we direct cattle. There will be a few more drives even after the railroad comes, but I've done it long enough. Time for a down payment on a ranch. Does ranch life appeal to you?"

"Life with you appeals to me."

"Sometimes ranch life is difficult – keeping cattle healthy, well-fed and watered. But we'll have each other." Paul handed Miranda a box of candy. "Caramels."

"I love caramels." Miranda didn't want to let go of Paul when the stagecoach came, but she finally did. The driver took her bag, and Paul helped her step up. Mr. Chadwick rode across from her, and she offered him a caramel.

"No thank you, Dear. My teeth are sensitive." Soon, the horses moved and they began their long ride to Eagle Ford.

"I brought some boiled eggs for us." Miranda held up her smaller traveling bag.

"And I brought sausage sandwiches." Mr. Chadwick smiled. "We should eat well on our trip."

Miranda looked outside the window. The Trinity River, numerous creeks, cedar trees, oak trees. Wilderness between the settlements of Fort Worth and Dallas. Despite the bumps in the road, Miranda fell asleep. She hardly slept the night before the trip, pondering whether or not to marry Paul.

She awoke, feeling hot. Chadwick handed her a water canteen, and she drank a big gulp.

"Are you ready for a sandwich?" Chadwick held up a sausage sandwich.

"Thank you. I have some boiled eggs here. Diana, our cook, already salted and peppered them."

"Just the way I like them." Chadwick accepted two eggs.

After they ate, Chadwick began talking. "You'll really like Dallas, Miranda. The railroad keeps it growing and growing. It does not look like much yet, but soon it will have beautiful buildings and an opera house. Dallas isn't as wild as Fort Worth. You can meet a nice young man there."

"I'm engaged to marry Paul, Mr. Chadwick. We hope to settle down in Bosque County, on a ranch."

"Ranch life is difficult."

"I know how to take care of cattle, Sir."

They were silent for the rest of the stagecoach trip. Finally, they arrived in Eagle Ford.

"I bet you haven't ridden a train before." Chadwick helped Miranda step down from the stagecoach.

"No Sir, I haven't," she answered.

She looked up at the enormous black engine while Chadwick arranged for the tickets. Once inside the coach, she was amazed at the luxury – red velvet curtains, plush leather seats, foot rests. The smell of new leather.

"Before long, you'll be able to ride the train from Fort Worth to Dallas," Chadwick said. "The stagecoach will be part of history."

"Yes, Sir."

Soon Miranda could see the three-story buildings of the Dallas skyline. She was almost disappointed because she enjoyed feeling the vibration of the powerful engine.

As the train stopped at the depot, Miranda saw a smiling tall man standing on the boardwalk.

"Hello, Mr. Graham," Chadwick said.

"And this must be my beautiful little sister," Graham said to Miranda.

"I'm pleased to meet you, Mr. Graham."

"Just call me Carl."

Carl took Miranda's large bag and helped her into his imperial carriage. Instead of sitting himself at the perch, in order to drive the horses, Carl sat next to his sister-in-law. Before she could protest, he kissed her on the mouth and tried to put his hand up her dress. She shoved him away, smoothed back her dress.

"Stop, Carl!" Miranda blushed. "You're married to my sister!"

"Why not?" He smirked. "You're already ruined."

"I am not ruined!" Her cheeks reddened in anger. "I'm engaged to be married!"

Miranda's Exile
Texas Star
episode 12

TEXAS STAR

"Welcome home!" Miranda's sister ran toward her with open arms as Miranda walked through the door. "This is your home now!"

"It's good to see you, Clotilda, but I'm engaged to be married." Miranda handed her sister her bonnet.

"Well, what a surprise. You just met someone, and already you're engaged to him!"

Miranda ignored her sister and hugged her mother.

"Thank God you're still alive!" Mama said.

A curly haired toddler ran to Miranda, and she picked him up. "What's your name?"

"His name is Andrew," Clotilda said.

"Andrew, can you say *Aunt Miranda*?" The little boy laughed.

"It's Andrew's bedtime. Let me put him down, and we all can sit and enjoy some lemonade. The railroad brings fresh lemons, so we can enjoy it nearly all year round." Clotilda left the parlor and returned with a tray bearing a pitcher and glasses. "I can't wait until the three of us go shopping together. There's this most marvelous store downtown – Sanger Brothers. That's where I found this dress."

Miranda looked at her sister's dress. It had a beautiful crocheted collar, but she could have sewn and crocheted it herself for half the price. "Very nice," she said without further comment.

"When you finish your lemonade, I want to show you the rest of the house. Right now, tell me about your beau."

"I met Paul during an emergency. A friend of mine needed a dentist. She was in a great deal of pain. He is a kind, gentle man who does not drink or smoke."

"What does he do for a living?" Mama

asked.

"He drives cattle North. He's saved most of his money. We plan to buy a ranch and settle down in Bosque County."

"And you've only known him a week!" Clotilda moved closer to Miranda. "Have you seen his bank statement?"

"No, I haven't seen his bank statement, Clotilda, but I have no reason to disbelieve Paul. Please don't judge until you've met him." Miranda finished the last of her lemonade.

Clotilda inhaled and exhaled impatiently. "We won't talk about Paul right now. Come see the house!" She rose and the other two women followed. "The kitchen is this way. It's the least interesting place in the house, but at least we have an ice box and a big-enough stove. A girl comes in and cooks. She helps me clean, also." Clotilda opened the ice box door and showed her sister the big block of ice, meat, and vegetables.

"Very modern," Miranda remarked.

"I can't wait to show you your room." Clotilda turned and led her sister and mother upstairs. She opened a door, lit a kerosene lamp, and pointed to the bed.

"What a lovely star quilt!" Miranda said.

"Remember when we were traveling from Alabama to Texas?" Clotilda asked. "We passed by a post office, and you saw the Lone Star flag for the first time. You thought it was the most beautiful flag you had ever seen. That's why I made you a quilt that resembles it."

"That arduous journey was so long ago, but I do remember the flag. And of course herding the sheep."

Clotilda laughed and picked up a small stuffed sheep from the dresser. "We can go to Sanger Brothers tomorrow and find a print for the wall. My treat."

"I love this room. Truly," Miranda said. "Does Mama stay here too?"

"No, I'll show you Mama's room. It's next door."

"Come look at my quilt," Mama said.

Miranda saw that a great amount of thought and planning had gone in designing and sewing her mama's flowered quilt also. *Despite all her arrogance, Clotilda does care for her mother. And me."*

"I'm about ready to turn in," Mama said.

"Go ahead," Clotilda said. "I want to get caught up with my sister." The two sisters returned to Miranda's room and sat in two rocking chairs.

"Miranda," Clotilda continued, "Please don't feel afraid to share anything you need to share with me. I'm sorry that I seem skeptical about Paul. I'm sure I'll change my mind when I meet him." Clotilda paused and looked in Miranda's eyes. "Carl does not know this, so please don't tell him. When I first came to Dallas, I had to sell myself in order to survive."

Civilized
Miranda's Exile
episode 13

CIVILIZED

In the morning, everyone sat at the mahogany table in the dining room, finishing their meal. The noise of the forks and knives on china plates diminished.

"It was so great meeting you, Miranda," Carl said, wiping his mouth on the napkin. "I'm going on a business trip, and I won't be back for two weeks. Hope I'll see more of you when I return."

"Have a safe trip," Miranda said, a little stiffly. She was relieved that Carl would be gone. The night before, she was prepared to scratch his face if he had come into her bedroom. Now, she could enjoy her breakfast hotcakes.

"Would you like any more cakes, Miss Miranda?"

"No, thank you, Naomi," Miranda said to her sister's cook. "But you make the best hotcakes I've ever tasted. I'm quite full right now."

"Thank you, Miss Miranda." She began to clean the dishes from the table. "Anything else that you need, just let me know."

Clotilda pushed her plate toward Naomi. "Do you mind looking after Andrew while I take Mama and Miranda to town?"

"No Ma'am. That'll be just fine." Naomi took Miranda's plate.

"And don't bother about fixing lunch." Clotilda rose from the table. "We'll eat at a restaurant."

"You ladies have a nice time," Naomi said, leaving the room with an armload of breakfast ware.

As the three women left the house, Clotilda explained, "It's such a nice day. Let's take the streetcar instead of a cab. I bet you've never ridden a streetcar, Miranda."

"No, but there are plans to bring one to Fort Worth, after the railroad comes to town."

"Dallas is ahead of Fort Worth by leaps and bounds!" Clotilda laughed as they walked toward the streetcar line.

Miranda admired the colonial houses as they passed.

Once they sat down inside the mule-driven vehicle, Clotilda commenced as a travel-guide: "Dallas is such an extraordinary town. It has a two-story limestone courthouse, a city park, and an iron bridge over the Trinity."

"I saw the iron bridge as I rode in on the rail," Miranda said. "Fascinating construction."

"How about churches?" Mama asked. "Do you go to church?"

"We sometimes attend the First Methodist Church."

"Methodist? That's too much like the Papist Church."

"We worship the same Jesus Christ, Mama," Clotilda laughed. "And such lovely people go there, including Mrs. Sarah Cockrell whose construction company built the iron bridge – and half of Dallas! She's one of Carl's best customers."

"A woman?" Mama asked.

"A gracious and brilliant widow," Clotilda said. "Oh, I forgot to tell you. Dallas has an opera house, also. Perhaps you two would like to see a show sometime."

"Dallas already *has* one of those?" Miranda asked, "The Pinkerton man said that it would *soon* have an opera house."

"He was mistaken. Dallas has had an opera house about three years now. At least some of our entertainment is civilized. I must admit, though, we almost turned into Fort Worth last year when that crazy woman – Belle

Starr – rode past the courthouse astride her plumed horse."

"I don't think Belle Starr has ever been to Fort Worth," Miranda said.

"Then she'll probably ride in with the first railcar!" Clotilda quipped. "Then maybe she'll stay away from Dallas!"

Before Miranda could defend Fort Worth, a policeman ran into the street.

"*Stop!*" he yelled. "Trouble up ahead!"

"You can't stop mules!" the conductor said.

"Here," the officer said and held the reins.

"What happened?" the conductor asked.

"A shootout at one of the saloons," the policeman explained. "You'll have to wait until the undertaker removes the bodies."

So much for the great civilization of Dallas!

Miranda thought.

Miranda's Exile
episode 14
Claddagh
Lace
Cate Murray

CLADDAGH LACE

Miranda felt a tension in her stomach as she and the others waited for the streetcar to move. One of the mules shook her head in impatience.

“We should be downtown soon,” Clotilda whispered. “We’ll purchase so much merchandise, I’ll have to arrange to have the packages delivered.”

“It’s wise to limit the spending.” Mama wiped perspiration from her forehead with a handkerchief.

“I’ll limit it later, but today we’re celebrating. Besides, my husband owns a lumber yard. Dallas is growing!”

The streetcar reached downtown Dallas as a hearse moved slowly ahead of them.

Miranda noticed that even Clotilda's mood sobered until the hearse was out of sight. *Dallas certainly has plenty of saloons, and saloons encourage heavy drinking. Unfortunately, heavy drinking sometimes leads to violence, no matter which city.*

Her first impression of the Sanger Brothers' Store was that the outside looked like an ordinary general store. But the inside revealed singularity and planning.

A bow-lipped young woman in a blue silk dress smiled as she held open the door. "Welcome to Sanger Brothers, Mrs. Graham."

"Nancy! How lovely to see you," Clotilda said, "I want you to meet my mother, Mrs. Davis, and my sister, Miranda Carr."

"How do you do, Mrs. Davis and Miss Carr. We have shipments of new merchandise this week, and I'll be glad to show you anything you want."

"Pleased to meet you, Nancy," Miranda said. "Do you sell lace?"

Nancy's smile bloomed even larger. "Come with me. I took a trip recently to England, France, and Ireland to purchase items. I'm very proud of the lace collection. I keep it hidden away from most customers, but I trust you to touch it." Nancy opened a drawer behind a display case and brought out a collection of handmade lace.

Miranda looked at Clotilda, and she almost laughed at her sister's raised eyebrows. *She wants to say something about my plans to marry Paul, but she won't speak about it in public.*

"Here is the very finest: Honiton Lace from Devon, England. It's the same lace as Queen Victoria's wedding gown back in 1840."

Miranda admired the flowered lace without touching it. "Indeed it *is* beautiful, but I'm afraid I can't afford it. Do you have some beautiful but less expensive lace?"

"Certainly," Nancy said. "I think this Alencon Lace from France is even prettier than the Honiton Lace."

"I agree with you. The flower patterns on the Alencon Lace look even daintier. I even like the buttonhole stitches. How much per yard?"

"Five dollars," Nancy answered.

"Thank you so much for your time, Nancy." Miranda turned to look at fabrics.

"Wait Miss Carr," the saleslady answered. "May I ask if this lace is for a wedding dress or veil?"

"Yes, Ma'am."

"Then I know exactly what you're looking for. And at the right price, too." Nancy pulled out a different drawer. "This lace is from Ireland. The pattern is called the Claddagh."

Miranda nearly burst into tears admiring the Claddaghs on the lace.

Nancy continued, "The heart, of course, symbolizes love. The two hands are those of the bride and the groom, and the crown signifies loyalty."

“Put it on my bill,” Clotilda said. “How many yards do you want, Miranda?”

“Four please.” Miranda was shocked that her sister agreed to buy the wedding lace for her.

“Congratulations,” Nancy said as she measured the lace. “Do you have the date set?”

“Not yet,” Miranda answered. “My fiancé is on a business trip.” *I suppose it is honest to describe a trail ride as a business trip. I should tell the complete truth because cowboy work is low-status but honorable!*

As they left the store, she held the sacked box containing the lace close to her chest.

Miranda's Exile
episode 15
Letters from Ft. Worth
Cate Murray

LETTERS FROM FT. WORTH

Soon after Miranda packed away her new lace, Naomi brought two letters to her. One letter was from Paul and the other was from Madam Porter. Miranda read Paul's letter first.

Dearest Miranda,

By the time you receive this letter, I will already be on the trail. I miss you, but I am glad you get to visit with your family. Hopefully, I will get to meet the members soon.

Have you ridden much? If not, I can teach you. When we have our ranch, I will need you to help me herd cattle. Also, side-saddle is rather dangerous, so I hope you don't mind riding straddle, while wearing a riding skirt.

Mrs. Porter has been kind and generous to both of us, yet I want you to stay elsewhere. Perhaps you can stay with your sister until we are ready to get married. If not, there are more respectable boarding houses for women.

I want to marry you as soon as I purchase the ranch, but I'll understand if you need to wait a bit longer.

I wrote the Fort Worth lady who is giving the ball and gave her our polite regrets. I look forward to attending balls in Bosque County with you. At least one lady, a Mrs. Nichols, gives balls and suppers in Bosque County. Perhaps we can do the same after we build the limestone house.

Love, Paul

Miranda kissed the letter and placed it in the top drawer of the dresser with her handkerchiefs. She then opened Madam Porter's letter.

My dear little Miranda,

I hope you are well and enjoying the visit with your family. We miss your lovely face and the beautiful piano tunes, but you are where you are supposed to be.

On July 19, the Texas and Pacific rail is

supposed to roll into Fort Worth. This event means good business for my house, but I am concerned about you. Railroad men tend to be rowdier than cowboys, and I cannot tolerate the idea of anyone saying anything rude to you.

I want to see you again, but perhaps you should find lodging somewhere else.

Enjoy Dallas. It has grown somewhat since I was last there.

I must watch Esther as if she were a child. She craves the drugs she took when her mouth gave her pain. She needs your prayers.

Know that you are in my prayers. Love, Mary Porter

How kind of her to write me and express her concerns, Miranda thought. She wanted to write to Paul, but she had no idea where to send a letter on the trail.

A knock on the door broke Miranda's reverie.

"Clotilda!" Miranda hugged her sister. "Once again, thank you for the lace."

"I saw your eyes light when you spoke of Paul, and I realized you love him. He must be an extraordinary man."

"I've never known anyone like Paul. As I said before, he doesn't drink, smoke, or gamble. He saves money rather than throwing it away like most cowboys. He has a way with horses, and I saw him calm a horse so that a blacksmith could shoe her."

"How old is Paul?" Clotilda asked.

"He's about 27 or 28. He was drafted into the war. Would you hold it against him if he fought for the Union?"

"No. We're all Union now. Besides, it was a foolish war. It could have been prevented."

"Some people are still fighting it, like Abner did." Miranda took the brush from the dresser and brushed her hair.

"I couldn't tolerate Abner's cruel words,

so I left home," Clotilda said. "Should have thought about you when I left you with the extra farm work."

"It's all in the past. You did what you had to do then."

The sisters heard a knock on the door. Miranda opened it, and Mama fell into her arms. With Clotilda's help, Miranda placed her mother into a chair and poured a glass of water from the glasses and pitcher on the bed table.

"Help me!" Mama's words were very audible. "My chest, my arm!"

"I'm going for the doctor!" Clotilda said and rushed from the room.

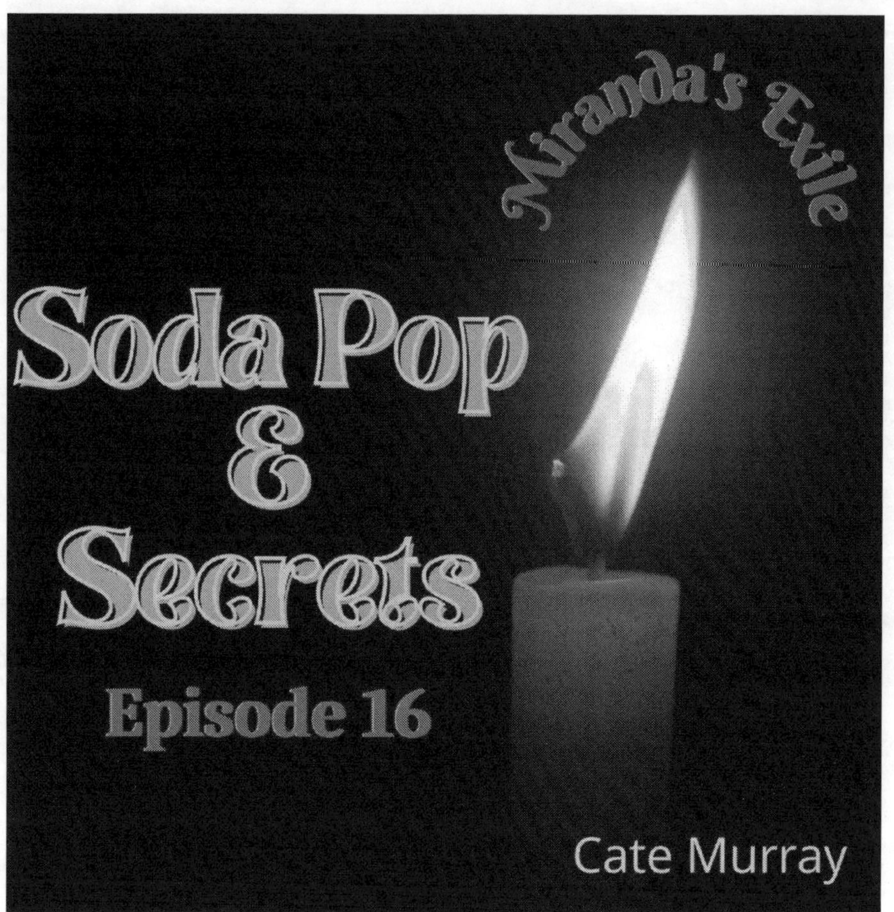
Miranda's Exile
Soda Pop
&
Secrets
Episode 16
Cate Murray

SODA POP & SECRETS

Miranda felt her mother's weak pulse. "Please don't die, Mama," she whispered. "The doctor will be here soon."

Thirty minutes later, a doctor and a nurse walked in without knocking. "You must leave," the nurse told Miranda. Miranda walked downstairs and found Clotilda holding Andrew and crying.

"You play with me," Andrew said to his aunt. He showed her some wooden toys and handed her a horse.

"What's this horse's name?" Miranda asked.

"Hoofer," the boy said.

"Hoofer, where would you like to go?"

"We may lose our mother," Clotilda said. "Has she ever had heart trouble before?"

"Not that I know of," Miranda said, "But Abner wouldn't allow either one of us to be sick."

"It's wrong to speak ill of the dead, so I won't say anything about our late stepfather. Would you like a soda pop? I asked Naomi to order some from the man that delivers the green groceries."

"Soda pop!" exclaimed Andrew. The two sisters laughed. Clotilda left the parlor and came back with three glasses on a tray.

"Here's your glass, Andrew." Clotilda handed her son a small glass. She then handed a larger one to Miranda and explained, "This soda doesn't have a name yet. It's a new concoction from a nearby drugstore, and the green grocer sells it."

Miranda tasted the cool, citrus drink. “Quite refreshing,” she said, then broke down crying. “I’m sorry!”

“What wrong?” Andrew asked.

“Don’t be sorry,” Clotilda told her sister. “She’s our mother. You’re closer to her than I.”

Andrew climbed into his aunt’s lap. “Don’t be sad.”

Miranda smiled. “You make me happy, but we need to do something about this sheep over here. He tries to run away.” She picked up the sheep and handed it to her nephew.

“Sheep, you stay with us. Don’t run away.” Andrew put the sheep next to the horse and yawned.

Clotilda silently mouthed, “It’s his bedtime,” lifted her son out of Miranda’s arms, and carried him upstairs.

When she came back down to the parlor, she said, “Since you’re getting married, I want to show you a secret. Clotilda handed Miranda a tubelike object. “This is a rubber, made by the B.F. Goodrich Company. If a man puts it on his tally-wacker before he enters a lady, the rubber prevents both disease and pregnancy.” Clotilda looked down. “I’m not sure Carl is faithful to me, especially on his business trips. He often returns smelling like perfume. I asked him to purchase a box of these. He thinks I want them to prevent pregnancy, but I really want them to forestall disease.”

“I’m sorry about Carl’s lack of judgment. You deserve better,” Miranda said. She felt of the rubber. “Isn’t it uncomfortable?”

“The rubbing sensation can be,” her sister answered. “So I have him use almond oil as a lubricant.”

This object—this rubber doesn’t seem very romantic. I guess the women at Mrs. Porter’s house use it. Hopefully, Paul and I will be able to afford all the children God gives us.

“Don’t you want more children?” Miranda asked.

“Oh yes! But only if Carl is healthy.

There are two basic types of the clap. There are treatments—silver nitrate and mercury, but they're both toxic. I don't want to lose him to a disease or a treatment..."

The doctor and nurse entered the parlor, noticed the rubber, and frowned judgmentally at the two sisters. The doctor's eyes moved from Miranda to Clotilda. "I'm sorry, Mrs. Graham," the doctor said, not displaying any emotion. "We weren't able to save your mother. Do you want to wash her yourselves, or do you want me to contact a funeral home?"

Miranda's Exile
Episode
Arrangements
Cate Murray

ARRANGEMENTS

Two men from a funeral home came and discreetly took Mama away.

"Your husband needs to sign if you wish to have her enbalmed," one of the men told Clotilda. She signed the paper explaining that her husband would be out of town on business for another week.

Clotilda looked at Miranda. "I realize other families have funerals in their homes, but I can't. I couldn't sleep with a deceased person under the same roof."

She and I both have experienced the death of animals on the farm, and we've been to funerals, but we haven't had anyone close to us die until now.

"I'll make a list of what we need to do tomorrow," Miranda said. "You need to send a telegram to Carl. He'll need to know about the expenses. And one of us needs to contact the church."

"Thank you. I wish I had bought Mama a new dress at Sanger Brothers, but I knew she would not have allowed me to indulge her. I guess we could choose what she called her Sunday-go-to-meeting dress. We can inter Mama in the Lisbon Cemetery. It's a lovely place and rather new."

Miranda and Clotilda both broke out crying. A few minutes later, a knock on the door interrupted their emotions. The sisters wiped their faces with handkerchiefs before Clotilda answered the door. "Mrs. Adams, please come in."

"I'm terribly sorry to bother you at this hour, Mrs. Graham, but I saw the hearse leaving." Mrs. Adams handed a basket to Clotilda.

Clotilda looked at the flowers and pie. "Thank you so much. Please sit down. It's our mother. Apparently her heart gave out."

"How do you do, Mrs. Adams. I'm Miranda, Clotilda's sister." Miranda shook hands with Mrs. Adams and sat down.

"Let me put the pie in the kitchen and find a vase." Clotilda carried the basket to the kitchen.

"Please to meet you, Miranda. It's a blueberry pie. The blueberries came in season mighty early this year. I made a half dozen pies this afternoon. Again, I'm terribly sorry about your mother. Have you made any arrangements?"

Clotilda re-entered the parlor. "Bradford Funeral Home."

"Bradford! Then you better have Mr. Graham handle the business. They'll charge a mint if a man's not with you. My widowed cousin employed them last year. She's still paying them!"

Clotilda sighed. "I'll telegram Carl tomorrow. Perhaps he can come home early. He's sold Bradford some wood, so possibly they will give us a respectable price for the services."

"Those Bradfords are from Philadelphia. Yankees! I hope you didn't agree to embalming?" Mrs. Adams face looked like she swallowed a lemon.

"Yes, I did. I'm not sure when the funeral will take place." Clotilda handed the empty basket back to Mrs. Adams.

Mrs. Adams moved closer to Clotilda. "Do you know how embalming is done? First, they take the naked body and soak it in arsenic..."

Miranda held up her hand to prevent Mrs. Adams from going on. Fortunately, Mrs. Adams excused herself soon after being silenced.

"I'm so sorry for having offended you. During the war, I volunteered in a Louisiana hospital, so nothing offends me." Mrs. Adams had a superior air about her lack of squeamishness.

"Thank you again for the daisies and asters and the pie. Miranda and I both love blueberries. I'll let you know when the funeral arrangements are made." Clotilda walked Mrs. Adams to the door.

After the front door closed, Clotilda told her sister, "Mrs. Adams, unfortunately, is the only lady at the First Methodist Church that I dislike. Actually, I don't think she's a lady at all. And she lives across the street!"

Miranda's Exile
Goldilocks
episode 18
Cate Murray

GOLDILOCKS

Dear Mrs. Porter,

Thank you for the beautiful letter. I would have written you back sooner, but my mother suddenly passed away. Apparently, she had heart trouble that neither Clotilda nor I knew about. We had a graveside service and buried her today.

I want to see you and the girls again, but perhaps you are right; I should live elsewhere. Paul and I plan to marry as soon as he purchases a ranch in Bosque County. He should return about July 4 – about the time we celebrate the American centennial. Perhaps we will see you then. It will be 15 days before the railroad's debut.

I will write again and keep you abreast of any plans. Love, Miranda

Miranda and Clotilda walked to the post office downtown, pulling Andrew in his stroller. Clotilda also had a letter to mail.

“Three miles is a great deal for me today,” Clotilda remarked. “Let’s take the trolley for the return trip.”

“Yes, six miles round trip would be hard on my feet.” Miranda agreed.

Andrew tried to climb out of his stroller, and his mother told him, “I’ll let you walk for a little while if you hold Aunt Miranda’s hand.” She turned back to Miranda. “The sidewalk ends here,” Clotilda explained. “Make sure Andrew doesn’t step near any horse paddies. A man cleans the street twice a day, but they still pile up.”

“Still, it’s nice that a city worker cleans the streets, and you have sidewalks around your neighborhood.” Miranda’s left hand felt sweaty, so she exchanged her left hand for her right hand to hold her nephew.

“Tell story,” Andrew asked his aunt.

“I’ll tell you a story about a little girl who believed she could have anything she wanted, even if it belonged to someone else."

"What the girl name?" asked Andrew.

"Goldilocks, because she had golden hair." Miranda proceeded to tell him the story of "The Three Bears." As they neared the downtown area, Miranda concluded the story. "Suddenly, Goldilocks awoke, saw the three bears, dove through the open window, and ran home." Miranda bent down to Andrew's face and asked him, "Do you think Goldilocks learned a lesson?"

Andrew frowned in concentration. "Yes. Don't sleep in bear beds."

"How about any beds that don't belong to you, unless the owner of the bed says you can sleep in it?" Miranda asked her nephew.

"And don't eat someone else's soup."

"Good, Andrew. What if you see someone else's candy, and you want it?"

"I say, please may I have some."

"That's better than just taking the candy. But it is better to wait until it is offered to you." Miranda helped Andrew step the big steps to the post office.

"Good morning, Mrs. Graham," the postmaster said. "Someone named Miranda Carr has a letter from Fort Worth, addressed to your residence."

"Mr. Holmes, this is my sister, Miranda." Clotilda took the letter from Mr. Holmes and handed it to her sister.

Miranda opened the letter from Esther.

Dear Miranda,

You are a special friend. Thank you so much for helping me when I had the toothache. I plan to pay you back the silver coins. I now have the most interesting teeth in Fort Worth! Right now, though, I need some more money. I have quit working at Mrs. Porter's house, and I am looking for respectable work. How I wish I could play the piano like you. Could you possibly send me a check for $10.00? I will pay you back before October. The *postmaster knows where to find me. Thank you for being such a wonderful friend, Esther.*

As Miranda, Clotilda, and Andrew waited for the trolley to ride back to the neighborhood, Miranda thought about Esther's letter. *She's probably hooked on drugs. If I don't send her money, she may start stealing. I just taught Andrew how stealing is wrong. But I really can't help her. She could take my money and steal anyway. She needs prayer instead. Lord, please help Esther quit drugs.*

Miranda made her decision.

Perhaps you can help her now, God, but I can't.

Cotton Tulle

"I've always wanted a full wedding dress, white and flowing with a bustle, no matter where or how the wedding is held."

Miranda's Exile

episode 19

Cate Murray

COTTON TULLE

The walk and the streetcar ride had caused Miranda to perspire profusely. She was thrilled when Clotilda suggested that they bathe first. Once she was in the warm bathtub, Miranda felt as if she were floating on a cloud as she luxuriated in the lavender-scented paradise.

Clotilda must have known her sister's thoughts as she knocked on the door. "I hate to disturb your reverie, but you have a telegram from Paul." Hearing Miranda get out of the tub, Clotilda said, "You don't have to hurry. The telegram will wait."

As soon as Miranda was dressed, she entered the parlor. When she opened the telegram, she read it aloud.

Leaving trail early. Found substitute. Arriving in Dallas Tuesday. Will stay in hotel. Love, Paul

"Well, aren't you the cat with the cream!"

Clotilda remarked.

"I have the cream but not the wedding dress," Miranda quipped. "I do have the pattern, though. At home, I worked as a seamstress, as you may recall."

"Do you want to follow Queen Victoria's tradition and marry in white?" Clotilda motioned for her sister to follow her. Miranda fell in step beside her.

"Yes, preferably white cotton tulle. The Claddagh Lace is made of cotton tulle." Miranda followed her sister to the sewing room.

Clotilda opened a box and lifted out a soft, white material. "This is for you. Ten yards, more than you need."

Surprised, Miranda felt of the material. "Perfect. But you bought it for yourself."

"I bought it to line the curtains. But I decided the curtain lining should be of heavier material. This cotton tulle is all yours now."

Miranda hugged Clotilda. "Thank you. I had

better start cutting the pattern."

"Do you plan to marry right away?"

"No, but I want to be ready for when the time arrives."

"Are there church buildings in Bosque County?"

"Probably not. Most of the rural areas only have circuit preachers."

"Then why are you sewing a dress for a formal wedding?" Clotilda spread the material on the table.

"This may seem silly to you, but I've always wanted a full wedding dress, white and flowing with a bustle, no matter where or how the wedding is held."

"Then you shall have whatever it is that you like, the way you want it. Let's dance!" Clotilda took her sister in her arms and twirled her around the small sewing room.

"We're free now," Miranda said. "Free of Abner, and we can dance! But I'm a bit dizzy because I'm not used to dancing." Miranda sat down.

"Let's not even mention his name then. I'm so happy for you. If you want to speed the sewing process, we can hire Mrs. Markham, the tailor's wife. She has a machine."

"A sewing machine! I've seen pictures of them, but I've never seen a real one."

"Let's have Mrs. Markham sew the dress on the machine, and you can sew the lace and put the finishing touches on it. Mrs. Markham also has the springs, wires, and mohair padding for the bustle. She's made most of my dresses."

"I love the calico one you have on, and the embroidery on your collar." Miranda looked at her sister's dress, imagining the pattern. Her concentration was interrupted by the doorbell. Clotilda and Miranda walked to the front door.

A woman with bobbed hair under her

hat and a riding skirt stood at the door. "Good evening to you two ladies. My name is Tamara Segal, and I would like to invite you to our next meeting of the Women's Christian Temperance Union. We are holding the event tomorrow night at seven o'clock, and we would like very much if you can attend."

episode 20
Hitch Up the Buggy
Cate Murray

HITCH UP THE BUGGY

As soon as Clotilda hung Tamara's hat on the rack, Tamara resumed her sales pitch for Christian Temperance. "Since the beginning of time, women have suffered from men's intemperance. Pouring liquor in their mouths have taken food away from the mouths of mothers and their children. Men receive their pay and celebrate right away in the saloon…"

"Miss Segal," Clotilda interrupted, "I'm tempted to offer you a glass of Sherry to calm you down."

"I wouldn't accept it, Mrs. Graham. I take my vow of temperance seriously. I know what alcohol can do. I've seen bruises on women and children. I've seen homeless women and children."

"Miss Segal," Miranda said. "My sister and I are both teetotalers. We realize that excessive drinking ruins many families. But some of the tactics of the WCTU are perpetuating the problem rather than eliminating it."

"What do you mean?" Tamara asked.

"Tactics such as going into saloons and destroying bottles of liquor with hatchets. That's worse than trying to catch flies with vinegar, so to speak. You are also destroying the livelihoods of bartenders and saloon owners."

"So how to you propose to eliminate the alcohol problem?" Tamara asked sarcastically.

"Education," Miranda answered. "Teach the dangers of excess alcohol in the schools. My teacher showed pictures of diseased livers. All teachers need to do the same."

"My husband drinks occasionally," Clotilda said, "But he's an excellent provider. Some people can handle alcohol."

"But most people can't," Tamara countered. "Do you believe Jesus turned water into wine?"

"Yes," said Clotilda. Miranda nodded.

"It was not wine! It was unfermented grape juice. The Bible translates it as wine, but it was not. The Lord sponsors the Women's Christian Temperance Union!"

Finally, Tamara realized that neither Clotilda nor Miranda were interested in forming a WCTU chapter in Dallas. She thanked them for their time.

#

The next morning Miranda sat with Andrew helping him draw pictures of horses. He held the pencil, and his aunt helped him guide it. A smiling Clotilda walked into the parlor and handed her sister a letter from Mrs. Porter and a telegram from Paul.

The telegram read *Let's go to Bosque*

County together. Until nuptials, you may stay with the Nichols family. Love

Miranda held the telegram to her heart, as she did with the last one. She opened Mrs. Porter's letter.

My Dear Miranda,

I hope you are well. All my girls are fine, except for Esther. I found her in an opium den. As soon as I could find someone to assist me, we placed her on a stagecoach for Bosque County. I had heard about an Indian woman there who treats people suffering from drunkenness. I pray that she can treat Esther's addiction also. Telegraphs were exchanged between the Bosque County sheriff's office and myself. The sheriff agreed to send a deputy to pick Esther up in a buggy and take her to the Indian woman's house.

I know you love Esther too, and I know you will pray for her. Since you and Paul plan to settle in Bosque County, could you check on her from time to time?

May God bless you and Paul as you begin your life together. Love, Mary

As Miranda mused over Mrs. Porter's

letter, Clotilda walked in with the box holding the white cotton tulle. She said, "I asked the handyman to hitch the buggy. Let's go to the tailor shop and arrange for your wedding dress to be sewn."

"Ca-an-dy!" Andrew said in three syllables.

"Yes, candy." Clotilda explained. "A candy store is next to the tailor shop."

"If you're good at the tailor's shop, I'll take you to the candy shop and buy you the candy," Miranda promised her nephew.

"Then you get candy too?" Andrew said.

Miranda and Clotilda both laughed.

WANTED
Bandits
After all, newsmen call this the Wild West for a reason.
episode 21

BANDITS

Two nights later

Sitting at the dining table, Paul held up his glass of ginger ale for a toast. "To this family: may the Lord bless us, keep us, and shine His light on us, guide us through obstacles, and remind us of His love."

Miranda, Paul, Clotilda, and Andrew had just finished a supper of roast beef and vegetables.

"That's a beautiful toast," Clotilda said. "I will miss you two when you leave tomorrow. How many stagecoach routes do you need to take?"

"A special friend of mine named Mr. Nilsen will gather us in his private coach," Paul said. "Bosque County is very rural—no stagecoaches. And the Houston and Texas

Central Railway travels southeast to Corsicana, not southwest to Bosque County, so we must depend on horses."

"Horses!" Andrew said.

"He loves horses," Clotilda explained. "When he gets older, I'll take him east of town to the pony riding range where he can take lessons."

"Come to visit us in Bosque County. We'll saddle him up," Paul said.

"And I need to make some riding skirts for me," Miranda said. "I need to help Paul herd cattle."

"Excuse me for a minute," Clotilda said. She returned holding up a brown riding skirt. "This is for you, Miranda. I have two of them, and I seldom ride any more."

"Thank you." Miranda stood up and held the skirt against her waist. "Looks like we still wear the same size."

"You are more than welcome to the skirt. Some of the women in this neighborhood would gossip if they saw me riding straddle," Clotilda laughed.

"Hopefully, the Bosque County ladies ride straddle themselves," Miranda said.

"The ones that ride do ride straddle," said Paul. "Side saddle is for society matrons and ultra-balanced women like Annie Oakley."

"But when Annie rode through Dallas, she rode straddle and every which way.

"I could never herd cattle side saddle," Miranda admitted.

"Nor would I want you to do so. Too dangerous." Paul said. "Bosque County people are practical. If anyone sees you riding straddle on you own property, no one would be scandalized."

The next morning, Mr. Nilsen arrived early.

He must have ridden during the night in order to arrive so soon. The horses were treated to hay, oats, and plenty of water while Paul loaded the coach. Clotilda handed Miranda a lunch basket of fried chicken and biscuits.

"I realize your Clydesdales are sturdy, but can they make the round trip?" Paul asked Mr. Nilsen.

"I've made an arrangement with a farmer who lives on the edge of Johnson County," Mr. Nilsen answered. "I'll trade my Clydesdales for some of his. We'll trade back at a later time."

Miranda and Paul felt relieved that the horses would not be overworked. She settled into a comfortable position determined to enjoy the long ride. *A long ride to a happy destination.*

As the coach traveled away from Dallas, Paul said, "I'm not good at keeping secrets."

"Then tell me one," Miranda said.

"I've known Mr. Nilsen for years. I herded his cattle on the trail. His son joined us one year, but he got seriously injured. I took care of him before he died. The other cowboys and I had to bury him in southern Kansas. Mr. Nilsen was so grateful, he wants to will his ranch to us. I told him I would check with you first."

"He is indeed a wonderful man," Miranda said. "Is Mr. Nilsen's ranch profitable?"

"Yes. A herd of 250 healthy cattle. He's had some trouble with wolves and coyotes, but I plan to purchase two donkeys to deter them."

"I've heard about donkeys deterring predators," Miranda said.

"Large donkeys can even kill coyotes. The jacks I plan to buy are the big kind. I'll have to keep them in a pen away from the cattle for a few days until the different creatures become accustomed to each other."

Four hours later, the group settled under a large oak tree to eat the chicken lunch. From a distance, two men on horses galloped near the tree. Miranda could see their noses and mouths were covered with bandannas. Mr. Nilsen grabbed for his pistol.

“Not so fast, old feller.” one of the men drawled. “We need no harm. Got any money?” The man pointed his pistol in the group’s direction.”

Paul threw a bag to the other man, and he caught it. “Got anything else of value?” the other man asked. He got off the horse and rummaged through the back of the coach. He grabbed the box continuing Miranda’s wedding dress.

“Please, not my wedding dress!” cried Miranda.

The men tied the box behind one of the saddles, laughed, and rode away

“I’ll buy you another,” Paul whispered. “The bag I threw him contained more dimes than dollars. The real money is hidden away!”

Miranda realized then that things would not always go so smoothly as she had imagined. She’d looked forward to wearing that special dress on her wedding day, but she knew the incident could have gone much worse.

After all, newsmen call this the Wild West for a reason.

A Rainy Rescue

As soon as Paul spoke, he and Miranda heard a clap of thunder. Seconds later, torrents of rain pounded the coach's top.

Miranda's Exile

episode 22

Cate Murray

A RAINY RESCUE

Miranda stood up from the picnic blanket. She felt her rapid heartbeat in her chest. *We all could have been killed! Lord, thank you for keeping us safe.* "Heavenly Father, we thank you for our lives. Thank you for sparing us from the outlaws' guns. Lord, soften the hearts of these bandits so that fewer people are threatened by them. We ask this in Jesus' name, Amen."

"That's a fine prayer. I'm sure the Lord heard it." Paul helped Miranda step inside the coach, and the journey resumed. Miranda tried to focus on happy thoughts. She admired the fields of black-eyed susans. Yet, she was perspiring more than usual. It was a hot day, but the water on her hands and face was mainly from nervousness. Miranda took a handkerchief and a folded fan from her bag, dabbed her face, and began fanning herself.

"You'll love Mrs. Nichols." Paul said.

"Everyone loves her. She's the most hospitable lady I know, and she's not a Southern lady. The Nichols are from New York."

Miranda looked at a boy swinging from an oak tree branch. "I look forward to meeting Mrs. Nichols. Does she have any children?"

"She has one boy about 11. His name's Eddie, and he has a great personality. When the other cowboys and I would ride through the area near the Nichols' property, Eddie would deliver fresh biscuits to us. After days of nothing but beans and hardtack, you have no idea how delicious fresh biscuits taste! And Mrs. Nichols has a special recipe."

"Didn't you say that the Nichols family gives balls and suppers?"

"Yes, and I bet Mrs. Nichols will give a ball for us before long." Paul placed his arm around Miranda. "She particularly likes old dances like the Virginia Reel."

"I've never heard anyone who wasn't from the South have an affinity for the Virginia Reel," Miranda laughed.

"The Nichols familycombines the best of North and South. They are all true Americans. There are a few people in Bosque County still fighting the War Between the States, but not many. Most of the people there are fine folks. "

Miranda steered the conversation back to the subject of dancing. "Wasn't the Virginia Reel adapted from an old English country dance?"

"I think it's adapted from Scottish country dances," Paul answered.

"I want to repay Mrs. Nichols' hospitality by helping her around the house as much as possible."

"She will appreciate your help. Mrs. Nichols is always nursing the sick and cooking for newcomers." Paul paused, then added, "We should be approaching the DePorter farm soon. Where Mr. Nilsen will receive a change of horses, remember?."

As soon as Paul spoke, he and Miranda heard a clap of thunder. Seconds later, torrents of rain pounded the coach's top. About a mile later, Miranda and Paul saw a small deer struggling in barbed wire. Paul pounded on the wall of the coach, signaling for Mr. Nilsen to stop. Paul ran to the deer and, careful not to face it directly, extricated the animal from the barbed wire. The fawn took off in a flash as soon as it was free.

Paul returned to the coach soaked. Mr. Nilsen, wearing a canvas coat, handed him two towels as he got inside. "I always travel prepared," Mr. Nilsen said.

"Thank you," Paul said as he dried himself. When Mr. Nilsen resumed the journey, Paul explained to Miranda, "A herd of deer likely became spooked by the thunderstorm. They jumped over the fence, except for the calf. I was afraid the coyotes or wolves would get him if I didn't rescue him."

"You are so brave and generous, Paul." Miranda hugged him despite getting wet herself.

Paul shrugged. "Rescuing animals in thunderstorms is nothing for cowboys. It's just one of the things that you have to do."

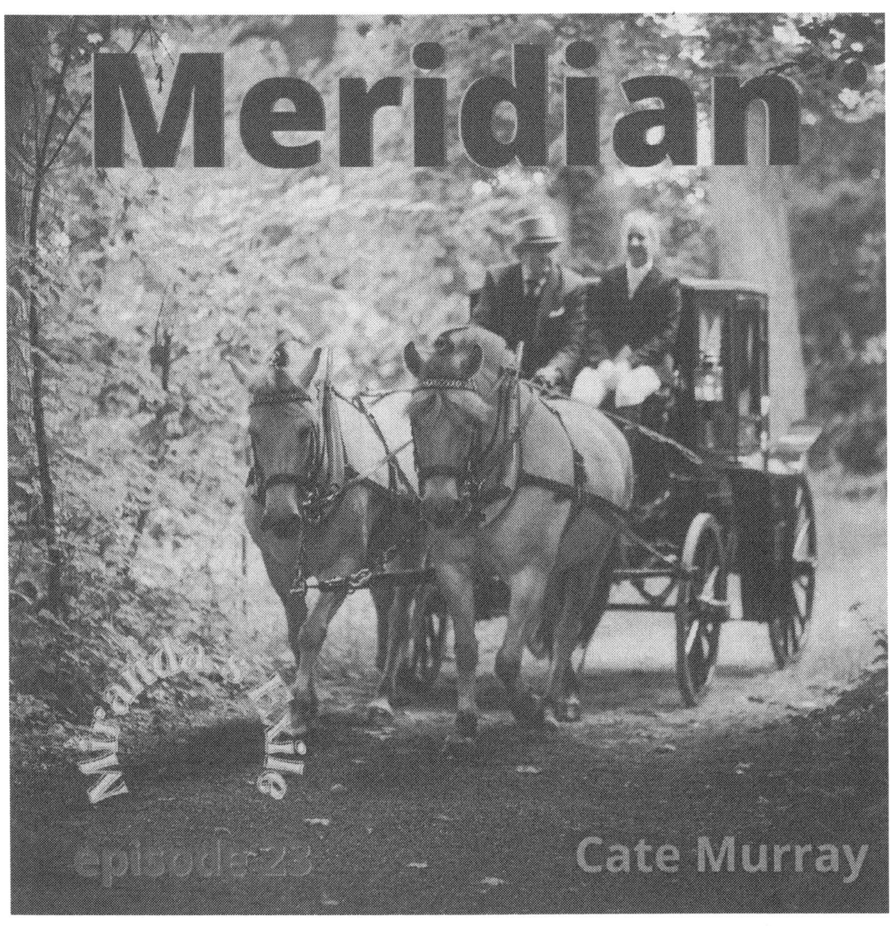
Meridian
Miranda's Exile
episode 23
Cate Murray

MERIDIAN

The horses were grateful for the hay and the dry barn, and Miranda felt relieved by dry clothes and a basket of sandwiches and peaches at the DePorter farm.

Paul showed Miranda a telegram. "It looks like you'll be staying in Meridian with Mrs. Nichols. She and the children had to leave the homestead at Steele's Creek sooner than expected. It's a temporary situation. She arranged to rent the homestead to another family while she and the children moved to Meridian so that they could attend school."

"How far is Meridian from the homestead?" Miranda asked.

"About eight miles, but the road is good."

"You folks are welcome to spend the night here," Mr. DePorter said.

Miranda and Paul looked at Mr. Nilsen.

"I'm prepared to go to Meridian this evening," Mr. Nilsen said. "The sun's fading, but it's still shining. I thank you for the offer, though."

Miranda and Paul both thanked Mr. DePorter and shook hands with him, and resumed the journey west toward Bosque County. The newly hitched Clydesdales picked up their step. Miranda put her head on Paul's shoulder. She didn't feel energetic like the horses did.

Paul took on the role of tour guide. "About 25 miles from here, in Erath County, is Chalk Mountain. I'll take you there some time. I've ridden past it, but I've never climbed it. The so-called chalk is probably limestone. As you see, limestone is plentiful in this part of Texas."

"If I go mountain-climbing with you, I'm sewing myself some pants," Miranda laughed.

"Or maybe you could just shorten a riding skirt," Paul said.

While Miranda admired some Queen Anne's Lace wildflowers, she heard a young boy shout, "Howdy Mr. Nilsen! I'll ride with you on the way to Meridian."

Mr. Nilsen stopped the coach long enough to introduce Miranda to Eddie Nichols. "Howdy do, Miss Carr. I heard you're quite a seamstress," Eddie said.

"I'm pleased to meet you, Eddie," Miranda said. "If you like, I'll make you an embroidered shirt."

"I'd be mighty pleased, Ma'am." Eddie's Palomino horse trotted along with the coach. "It won't be long before we reach Meridian."

"According to Bosque County legend," Paul said, "Eddie could ride before he could walk. He's the most personable boy I've ever known. About eight years ago, some Tonkawa Indians settled on Steele Creek. The women even let Eddie play with their babies."

"I'm sure Mrs. Nichols is proud of her son," Miranda said.

"If I remember correctly, Mrs. Nichols has an older son and some daughters. I haven't met them yet, though."

Miranda managed to doze while the horses pranced. When she awoke, Paul told her that they were passing the Nichols' homestead at Steele Creek. He pointed out a two-story rock home with a large veranda."

"Beautiful," Miranda said.

"At the rate these horses are running, we'll be in Meridian in an hour," Paul said, then added, "We're about 22 miles from the ruins of an old military fort, Fort Graham. If you like, I'll take you there some time. When we stood at the ruins of Fort Worth, I told you about Major Ripley Arnold, didn't I?"

"Yes. I think that was when I waited for the Dallas stagecoach," Miranda answered.

"Yes. Unfortunately, Major Ripley Arnold lost his life to a doctor at Fort Graham. Arnold tried to arrest Dr. Steiner for drunk and disorderly conduct, but the doctor got angry and shot him."

"That's terrible behavior for a doctor. I'd like to see what's left of Fort Graham, though. Tell me about Meridian." Miranda straightened her bonnet.

"Meridian is the county seat of Bosque County. It has a log cabin for a court house, but there are plans to build a larger one. Some of the homes there are more modern than the court house."

Night had fallen by the time the coach reached the Nichols' Meridian home. A friendly collie dog greeted the group, and Mrs. Nichols called from the veranda, "Come inside. I am so happy to see you. I'll warm some plates so that you can eat supper."

Everyone stepped down from the coach, tired and grateful for the trip's ending.

Eddie got off his horse, flapped his hat and said, "I'm starving."

Apprehension
Miranda's Exile
Cate Murray
episode 24

APPREHENSION

Miranda slept well in the feathered bed and rose when she heard children's voices and dogs barking. She dressed quickly.

"Good morning, Miranda," Mrs. Nichols said as she rushed around the dining room. "Your fiance and Mr. Nilsen left earlier. The hens haven't been laying many eggs lately. How about a piece of pie for breakfast?"

"Pie for breakfast would be luxury!" Miranda answered.

"Peach or mock apple?" Mrs. Nichols pointed to two different stacks.

"I'll try a mock apple." Miranda sat at the table. "I've heard of mock apple pies, but I've never tasted of one. I wonder who invented them."

"During the War between the States, the Southerners missed their apple pies, so a lady in Georgia decided to cut crackers like apple slices and season them with cinnamon and sugar." Mrs. Nichols sat the piece in front of Miranda.

After Miranda had chewed and swallowed her first bite, she remarked, "This is delicious."

"Not as scrumptious as real apple pie, but when you can't get apples, improvise." The hostess sat a coffee cup before Miranda and sat down across from her with her own coffee cup. "I am so glad Paul found a gracious, beautiful young lady. I look forward to showing you around Meridian and introducing you to my friends."

"I look forward to meeting your friends, Mrs. Nichols. Do any of them have a dry goods store where I can buy some material to sew my wedding dress?"

"Mr. and Mrs. Evans have quite a nice dry goods store, but Paul told me you already had your wedding dress. He told me in a brief telegram." Mrs. Nichols cleared the table.

Miranda looked down. “Two bandits robbed us somewhere in south Dallas County or north Johnson County. But they didn't hurt us. They took the dress and some money.”

“Thank God those criminals didn't harm any of you! I'm sure they'll try to sell the wedding dress. Was it very distinctive?”

“The dress itself isn't unique, except that it is solid white. I also had some Irish lace in the box in the Claddagh design. I had planned to adorn the dress with the lace.”

“Wait a minute,” Mrs. Nichols said. “I have something to show you.” She left the room and returned with a gold ring with the hands-and-heart Claddagh design. “Mr. Nichols gave this ring to me before we were married. Our jeweler, in New York, was Irish.”

“Did you wear this ring as an engagement ring?”

“Yes I did, and I've hardly worn it since the wedding ring replaced it.” Mrs. Nichols took

Miranda's left hand and placed the Claddagh ring on her ring finger. She explained, "You wear the heart upside down before you're married, and afterwards, you turn the ring around."

"Beautiful." Miranda started to remove the ring.

"If you want it, it's yours. I'm sure Paul won't mind."

"Mrs. Nichols, I love it! You are so generous and gracious. At least let me help you with dishes."

"You are generous and gracious yourself. I'll let you help me with dishes. I gave my kitchen help a week off. Her name is Bettina and she has a new grandchild."

"How lovely," Miranda said as she took a damp cloth from Mrs. Nichols, and wiped the table.

"Mama! Good morning, Miss Carr." Eddie's face was sun-flushed. He took off his hat and hung it. "The Hill County constable caught two reprobates trying to cross the Brazos on the ferry. Sheriff Careton is holding them in the jail. He's here to speak to Miss Carr."

Miranda felt her heart jump. A man with a badge came to the door, and Mrs. Nichols opened it. She introduced Sheriff Careton to Miranda.

The sheriff opened the box. "Is this yours, Miss Carr?"

Guardian
Donkeys
Miranda's Exile
Cate Murray
episode 25

GUARDIAN ANGELS

Miranda looked inside the box and rejoiced. The lace and the dress were both there. "Thank you so much, Sheriff!"

"You are welcome! It's truly my pleasure to bring good news. It gets around town when a couple is getting married, so I figured the white dress and lace would be yours." Sheriff Careton put his hat back on his head.

"You're welcome to stay and have some coffee," Mrs. Nichols offered.

"Some other time, Ma'am. I've got to telegram some other sheriffs and determine if they're looking for the same men I'm holding." The sheriff looked at Miranda. "Young lady, I'm so glad neither of the thugs hurt you."

"Thank you, Sir," Miranda answered.

"God is good," Mrs. Nichols said, and everyone agreed. After the sheriff left, Elizabeth Nichols examined the Claddagh lace and lifted the white dress out of the box. "If you don't mind, I'd like to help you sew on the lace."

"I would be honored if you helped me."

"One thing I am superstitious about, though, is letting the bridegroom see the dress before the wedding day." Mrs. Nichols' face was serious.

"That's fine with me," Miranda said, "I want Paul to be surprised. She folded the dress back into the box. "Which room should we take it to do the sewing?"

"I've set aside a room in the back for sewing and reading." Mrs. Nichols led Miranda to a sunny room with a sewing basket and bookshelves. The room also had a small table with three chairs.

"Very nice," Miranda said. "The chairs are even padded with needlework cushions." She looked at the *fleur-de-lis* designs.

"I did the needlework myself. Since I'm part French, I'm fond of symbols of my heritage. I love French cooking, also. How would you like for me to bake your wedding cake?"

"How wonderful! Do the French have special ways of baking cakes?"

"They have special recipes and unusual decorations. I would truly enjoy baking and decorating your cake.

Miranda hugged Mrs. Nichols. Before they could commence sewing, they heard a knock on the door. Thinking Paul could be calling, Miranda closed the door to the room and followed her older friend to the front.

Mrs. Nichols opened the front door and greeted a friend. "Mrs. Speer, come in this house! This is my friend, Miranda Carr."

Mrs. Speer handed a basket of eggs to Mrs. Nichols and smiled at Miranda. "Pleased to meet you, Miss Carr. Mrs. Nichols, I heard your hens weren't laying. For some reason, my hens have been producing in excess.

"Thank you so much. Do you need any butter or sewing materials?"

"No, Ma'am. Mr. Speer and I are fine. I need to be heading back, though."

"I was hoping you could join us for a sewing party. Miss Miranda is engaged to be married."

"How blessed you are," Mrs. Speer said. "Is your fiancé anyone I know?"

Before either Miranda or Mrs. Nichols could answer, they noticed Paul at the door.

"Hello, Paul," Mrs. Speer greeted.

"It's great to see you, Mrs. Speer. I'm the potential bridegroom with two gifts for the future bride. Come outside and I'll show you, Miranda."

Miranda and the other two women followed Paul.

"Are they mules?" Miranda asked.

"No, mules don't guard pastures," Paul answered. "They are the largest donkeys I could find. They have proven their guarding skills, too. And we can ride them, they're sturdy enough."

"Thank you, Paul. I don't want wolves or coyotes to snatch our calves."

"Why don't you change to a riding skirt? I want to show you Mr. Nilsen's place, our place."

"Just get her back before sundown," Mrs. Nichols said.

"Yes, Ma'am," Paul answered.

Miranda hurried inside to change into her skirt, hoping she wouldn't make a fool of herself. She'd never ridden a donkey before.

A Chance Meeting
episode 26
Miranda's Exile
Cate Murray

A CHANCE MEETING

Miranda petted the donkeys before she mounted Maisie. Paul's mount was named Monte. "They're so gentle."

"I wouldn't want them any other way," Paul said. "Gentle with us, gentle with calves, but rough on coyotes. I also made certain these donkeys weren't kin to each other. A boy and a girl might decide to mate, and we don't want inbreeding."

"How wonderful! I've never seen a baby donkey."

"We already have three newborn calves."

"Paul, I'm excited to see the land and the cattle that will be ours someday, but we can't talk about it being ours yet. It isn't right."

"Mr. Nilsen told me he wants to will us the land as soon as we are married." Paul pointed to a hill that they needed to cross. "He's such a terrific friend. Do you mind if he lives with us?"

"Of course not. He's my friend too. I'll cook and clean for both of you." Miranda brushed her hair from her eyes.

"Watch for that rock over there." Paul saw the rock first.

"Thanks, Paul."

"Donkeys are more accustomed to big rocks in the path, but sometimes they become spooked by them." Changing the subject back to Mr. Nilsen, Paul added, "He is grateful to get help with his ranch. With his arthritis, it's hard for him to perform hard tasks, whether at home or on the ranch."

"Does Mr. Nilsen take any medicine for his arthritis?"

"He prefers folk remedies. A Cherokee Indian friend, Mrs. Espy Speer, introduced him to hot water treatment and herbal teas. To some extent, his pain has been alleviated."

"I met a Mrs. Speer yesterday. She was elderly and looked Indian. She brought some eggs for Mrs. Nichols."

"Sounds like the same Mrs. Speer," Paul said. Like many of the neighbors around here, she's more than generous." He paused then added, "Mr. Nilsen told me that she conducts prayer meetings for women who have fallen to heavy drink or drugs."

Should I mention Mrs. Porter's letter about Esther moving to Bosque County for treatment? No, I need to keep confidence for Esther. Even with Paul, Miranda thought.

"We're about a mile from the homestead," Paul said. "I built a special pen for the donkeys. It's temporary. The donkeys need to meet the cattle and Mr. Nilsen's dog. Once they get used to each other, they'll have a chance to bond. After they bond, the donkeys will protect the herd."

"Is it possible they won't bond?" Miranda asked.

"It's possible, but I picked friendly donkeys who have proved their guardian skills, so it's unlikely they won't bond with the herd. It may take a few days."

In the distance, a woman in a cowboy hat rode on a spotted horse. She waved, and Miranda and Paul recognized her as Maddie from Mrs. Porter's house. "What a surprise!" Maddie remarked.

"Good to see you! Are you living in Bosque County now?"

"Just for a while. I started to drink too much, and a lady is helping me recover. She's helping Esther too." Maddie wiped the perspiration from her forehead.

"You look good. How's Esther?"

"She's better. She talks about you all the

time. We're staying in an abandoned slave cabin. The rent's cheap, but we fixed it up nice. Come see us."

"I'd love to. Guess we need to head to our destination." Miranda and Paul turned their donkeys toward the homestead, and Maddie rode her horse in the opposite direction.

"Like any community, Bosque County has its gossipers," Paul said. "Be careful who you associate with."

"These women are friends who make mistakes."

"I agree. Just thought I'd warn you about gossips who see the faults of others rather than their own. Also, Maddie and Esther may go back to whoring when they think they are recovered enough."

Paul's words felt like a thorn in Miranda's heart. *How can he have so little faith in Maddie and Esther? Could he believe in once ruined, always ruined?*

4th of July
Miranda's Exile
episode 27
Cate Murray

4TH OF JULY

Miranda spun around in her wedding dress. "It's beautiful! Thank you so much for finishing it," she told Mrs. Nichols.

"I'm happy you like it. I was hoping you would be pleased rather than disappointed that I stepped in and finished it." Mrs. Nichols smoothed Miranda's dress in the back. "The Methodist preacher is in town for the Centennial celebration, and he said he would be glad to perform the ceremony within two days."

"Do any pastors live in Meridian?"

"Not yet, but hopefully one or more will settle nearby soon." Mrs. Nichols changed the subject. "Do you have a white bonnet?"

"No, I don't. Perhaps I could wear my blue one."

"Wait a minute. Let's see if one of mine works." Mrs. Nichols walked upstairs and came down with a hatbox. She opened it and pulled away yards of wrapping. "I haven't worn this hat for about five years. The wrapping keeps off the dust." Mrs. Nichols held up a sailor bonnet trimmed in artificial white roses.

"This is perfect for my wedding dress!" Miranda placed the hat on her head.

Mrs. Nichols looked at Miranda's reflection in the mirror. "We can tie it down with hairpins to make it secure." She took hairpins from the hatbox and pinned the hat on Miranda's head.

"I'm ready to get married in two days or less, if Paul is ready."

"Why don't I send Eddie out to find Paul and Reverend Matthews? Eddie has an uncanny way of finding people."

Soon after Mrs. Nichols spoke, a knock was heard at the door. To avoid Paul seeing her in the dress, Miranda lifted her skirt and climbed the stairs holding the hat box and wrappings. At the top of the stairwell, she paused to listen below.

"Paul!" Mrs. Nichols said. "Miranda and I were just about to send Eddie out to find you. Rev. Matthews is in town for the Centennial tomorrow, and he is willing to perform the wedding ceremony in the next two days."

"That's fine with me. I just need to purchase the ring. Is the wedding dress ready?"

"Yes. I finished it myself. Miranda's changing out of it, and she'll be downstairs shortly. I'll leave you two to tell secrets in the parlor." Mrs. Nichols winked.

"I'm blessed to have you as a friend, and I'm blessed to have Miranda," Paul said.

"I'll send Eddie to the house where Rev. Matthews is staying," Mrs. Nichols said. "The three of you can get together and set the date."

Miranda went into her bedroom to change back into her day dress.

The date was set as July 5th, the day after the

July 4th celebration. "So we're to be married on Wednesday, like Solomon Grundy in the poem," Paul joked.

"But you better not take ill on Thursday and die on Friday like Solomon Grundy!" Miranda answered.

Paul and Rev. Matthews laughed. Miranda couldn't laugh at just the idea of her beloved becoming ill and dying.

The pastor cleared his throat. "Let's see if I remember that rhyme. Ah...

Solomon Grundy, born on Monday,

Christened on Tuesday,

Married on Wednesday,

Took ill on Thursday,

Worse on Friday,

Died on Saturday,

Buried on Sunday,

That's the end of Solomon Grundy!

Miranda and Paul clapped. "I was wrong,"

said Miranda. "He died on Saturday, not Friday."

"Let's have happier words read at the wedding," Paul said.

"Absolutely!" Rev. Matthews said. "Some of the 'Song of Solomon' may be appropriate, but not 'Solomon Grundy.'"

"What's that ring on your hand?" Paul asked Miranda.

"So much has been happening, I forgot to tell you. It's an Irish claddagh. Mrs. Nichols gave it to me. Irish girls wear it upside down like this before they get married, and right side up after they are." Miranda started to tell Paul that the ring's design matched the lace on the wedding dress, but she decided to let the dress be a surprise to Paul.

"Beautiful," Paul said. "Would you like wear it with your wedding ring?"

"I think so. If they fit together."

The next day, July 4th, Miranda, Paul, Mrs. Nichols, and the pastor all stood across from the log cabin courthouse, waving American flags, and meeting Bosque County citizens. Mrs. Nichols announced the upcoming wedding and invited people to attend.

"Are you sure you want to marry her?" a man asked Paul. His face was glum. He stared at Miranda.

"Why not, Sir?" Paul asked.

"A couple of months ago, I was in Fort Worth. Saw her crossing Main Street into Hell's Half Acre."

False
Witness
Miranda's Exile
episode 28
Cate Murray

FALSE WITNESS

Paul placed his arm around Miranda. "I know this girl. She played the piano in an entertainment house in Fort Worth. A madam gave her the piano job when she was homeless. But she never worked there as a harlot!"

"I'd make certain if I were you," the man said and left.

Through tears, Miranda looked at Mrs. Nichols and Rev. Matthews, hoping that no one else overheard.

Mrs. Nichols hugged Miranda. "I believe Paul. You're my friend. He told me about your stepfather throwing you out and later getting himself killed."

"I think he shortened my mother's life," Miranda whispered. "She died shortly after he was killed."

Paul escorted Miranda, Mrs. Nichols, and the pastor to the drugstore and bought ginger ales for everyone.

"One of the Ten Commandments tells us not to bring false witness against our neighbors," Rev. Matthews reminded the group. "People judge and gossip before they know the truth."

Paul looked at Miranda. "Do you feel like going to the picnic at noon?"

Miranda smiled. "Certainly. I don't have anything to hide."

"Hold your head high," Mrs. Nichols said. "You deserve it."

Paul glanced at the clock on the wall. "May I borrow your claddagh ring for a while? I want to be certain your wedding ring fits."

"Why can't I go to the jeweler's with you?" Miranda asked.

"I want the ring to be a surprise." Paul winked, took the claddagh ring, and left.

Mrs. Nichols explained, "The jeweler had planned to close for the holiday, but he agreed to have one customer, Paul. Paul had saved one of his bulls from drowning a few years back."

"I love the way so many neighbors help each other here in Bosque County." Miranda wiped her perspiration with a handkerchief.

"Yes, most people here are good, generous, and hardworking." Mrs. Nichols paused. "The man who tried to insult you became bitter after his wife left him last year."

"Bitter people need prayer," the pastor said, and the two women agreed.

Rev. Matthews delivered the joyous invocation at the picnic in a shaded area near downtown Meridian. Miranda thanked God for her life in the United States. She had heard of countries where women suspected of prostitution were stoned to death. She looked around to try to see the man who had accused her but thankfully could not find him.

"I am so happy for you!" Mrs. Espy Speer said. "I want you to meet my grandson, Hubert. He goes by the nickname, Hub."

"It's so nice to meet you, Hub," Miranda said. "Are you coming to my wedding tomorrow?"

"Yes Ma'am." The blonde haired boy of about four grinned. "And my brothers and sisters." He pointed to the stage where school-aged children stood in three horizontal lines. Eddie led them in "The Star-Spangled Banner." Afterwards, Eddie recited Longfellow's poem, "The Midnight Ride of Paul Revere."

Everyone clapped afterwards, the pastor delivered another prayer, and lunch was served. Fried chicken, watermelon, pies, and cakes.

"Mrs. Steiner has a special recipe for potato salad," Mrs. Nichols said as she placed a serving on Miranda's plate.

"Just cake, no pies, Paul?" Mrs. Nichols said.

"Even I have my limits!" Paul laughed. "The food is all terrific."

"Miranda, you may end up tomorrow with wedding pies rather than wedding cakes," Mrs. Nichols told the bride-to-be.

"That would be fine with me," Miranda answered.

The crowd was still eating while the fireworks began. Firecrackers spooked two of the horses. They reared up, jerked themselves out of their tethers, and began running in the western direction.

"I better go catch them!" Paul stood up from the table and ran towards his own horse.

Wedding Day

the pastor performed the ceren
Nichols stood as Miranda's matr
or, and Eddie served as Paul's
. When Eddie handed the wed
to Paul, Paul placed it on Mira
er. He then took the claddagh rin
ed it above the wedding ring. Mir
ced that a tiny diamond was o
ding ring, and the bottom of the
ted to the diamond.

WEDDING DAY

Miranda was overjoyed after hearing that Paul had not been seriously injured while retrieving the horses, but melancholy later moved in like a tide. She felt sad that neither her late mother nor her sister could attend her wedding. Perhaps Clotilda might have attended if Miranda could have set the date later. She tossed and turned the night before, and sleep came only in the early morning hours.

Miranda awoke with Mrs. Nichols' voice, "Goodness! You don't want to miss your own wedding!"

"Paul would have to find someone else quickly if I don't show!" Miranda quipped.

Politely, Miranda ate a light breakfast although she didn't feel like eating.

"Miranda, all girls feel apprehensive on

their wedding day." Mrs. Nichols studied her face.

"I'm sure I'll feel better afterwards," Miranda said. "You're going to visit us at the ranch, aren't you?"

Mrs. Nichols hugged the bride-to-be. "I certainly will visit. And you are always welcome here. Eddie will help you catch any cattle that get loose. He's driving your groom to the church today."

"I guess it's time to slip into my dress now," Miranda said.

"I'll help you."

Mr. Nilsen came by as soon as Miranda was dressed. He drove the bride and her friend to the church. Well wishers stood on each side of the street a block from the church. They cheered, waving flowers in their hands. Esther and Addie were among them. Esther's silver teeth shone in the sun as she smiled. Next to Esther, little Hub Speer held up a bouquet of roses tied with ribbons.

"Hub Speer is the brightest four year old I've ever known," Mrs. Nichols whispered. "He can write the name of everyone in his family, and he can count at least to 200."

When the coach stopped at the church, Hub handed Miranda the bouquet that his grandmother had made. He kissed her on the cheek, and she returned the kiss.

Reverend Matthews met Miranda and Mrs. Nichols at the door. "It's a beautiful day. Not too hot."

Despite the cuts on his face and hands, Paul stood like a handsome beau at a dance. A lady played Bach's *Air on a G String* on piano, and Miranda took Eddie's arm. He led her to the front of the church.

As the pastor performed the ceremony, Mrs. Nichols stood as Miranda's matron of honor, and Eddie served as Paul's best man. When Eddie handed the wedding ring to Paul, Paul placed it on Miranda's finger. He then took the claddagh ring and placed it above the wedding ring. Miranda noticed that a tiny diamond was on the wedding ring, and the bottom of the heart pointed to the diamond.

The short sermon was based on the Book of Ruth from the Bible, one of Miranda's favorite books. Rev. Matthews read the lines, "Where you go, I'll go, and where you live, I'll live. Your people are my people, and your God is my God."

After the ceremony Miranda and Paul kissed and raced outside. They stepped into Mr. Nilsen's coach, Paul asked, "How do you feel being Mrs. McCart?"

"I feel grand!" admitted Miranda.

"I was wrong about my earlier feelings regarding Esther and Addie. They smiled at you with love in their eyes. You may keep your friendship with them."

Miranda hugged and kissed her new husband.

Mrs. Nichols hosted the reception. She had hired women to set the food on the tables while the wedding party was at the church. As people crowded around the couple well-wishing them, a man came by the house and delivered Paul a telegram.

"It's from my brother. I telegrammed him and told him about the wedding." Suddenly Paul's forehead showed concern. "He says he's sending his young son to us! Come with me into the kitchen."

Once his voice was out of earshot, Paul explained, "He says his wife will not accept the boy. I assume that a woman other than his wife is the mother."

Miranda started to protest, then remembered. *Your people are my people.*

"What do you think?" Paul asked.

"I'll take care of him. I love you," she answered.

Awaiting a Child
"Disciplining a child in a healthy way is something I'm going to have to learn. I just remember my stepfather saying, 'Some children you spank, and others you beat within an inch of their lives.'" Miranda shuddered.
Miranda's Exile
episode 30
Cate Murray

AWAITING A CHILD

Miranda and Paul rejoined the wedding reception, and Mrs. Nichols asked, "Is anything wrong?"

Paul showed Mrs. Nichols the telegram from his brother. "It looks like Miranda and I will have a son a few days from now. Hank doesn't say how old the boy is or what his name is."

After Mrs. Nichols read the telegram, she said, "It's possible that the boy may be unstable from being passed from relative to relative."

"As I told Miranda, the child is apparently from a woman other than my sister-in-law."

Mrs. Nichols hugged Paul and Miranda. "I commend you for agreeing to take in the boy."

"Knowing my brother, he has already placed his son on a train. Hopefully, he will let me know when and where to pick the boy up. We'll take him to the ranch, teach him how to ride, and love him."

"Love, rules, and consistency. Those ingredients worked with raising my family."

"We'll remember that, Mrs. Nichols," Miranda took her older friend's hand.

"I thought we'd wait at least a year to become parents, but I guess God has alternate plans," Paul said.

"He surprises us, but he knows best," Mrs. Nichols said.

After returning to their ranch, Miranda and Paul admired the sunset and the lavender clouds. *I wonder how many evenings will be serene like this after the boy arrives?* Miranda thought, then told herself, *I can't be selfish and want Paul all to myself. The Bible teaches that children are God's gift, and I must think of our new son as God's gift.*

"What are you thinking about?" Paul asked.

"Our son. How old is he? What interests him?"

"You are a fine Christian woman," Paul said, "to be thinking of others rather than just yourself."

"I have a long way to go spiritually, Paul. Just a while ago, I was lamenting the possibility that the sudden child might cause problems with our relationship."

"If a troubled child tries to come between us, we'll stick together and give him necessary discipline."

"Disciplining a child in a healthy way is something I'm going to have to learn. I just remember my stepfather saying, 'Some children you spank, and others you beat within an inch of their lives.'" Miranda shuddered.

"Stand up and dance with me, Miranda. We don't need music to dance. We're as one now. We can do all things through Him who gives us strength."

"I never learned how to dance."

"Just go limp in my arms."

Mr. Nilsen opened the front door and stepped onto the porch. "I hate to interrupt you, but I fixed a bite to eat."

Miranda wasn't hungry after the reception hours earlier, but she followed Mr. Nilsen inside. "I apologize for not helping you. I didn't realize you were fixing dinner."

"You shouldn't apologize," Mr. Nilsen said, "I'm just happy to help the new bride and groom."

After the prayer, Mr. Nilsen again spoke, "I will help you raise the boy. It's been many years since a young boy lived at this ranch. In some of the boxes, I still have toys I made for my sons."

Tears flowed from Miranda's eyes. "Mr.

Nilsen, I can't get over how kind you are. Just a few minutes ago, I was afraid of being a mother so soon after being married. You, Paul, and Christ give me strength."

"All strength comes from the Lord," Mr. Nilsen said.

They heard a knock at the front door, and Paul answered it.

"We just came by long enough to deliver the gifts," Esther said. "We made them ourselves." She held up a pair of blue baby booties.

Addie held up some yellow booties. "We heard that your nephew will arrive soon. I don't know how old he is, though."

"We don't know how old he is, either," Paul said. "But thanks, I'm sure we'll need booties sooner or later." He winked at Miranda.

Wedding Night
Miranda's Exile
episode 31
Cate Murray

WEDDING NIGHT

"Let's don't be shy with each other," Paul said as he and Miranda faced each other in their nightclothes.

"I'm a little nervous," Miranda admitted.

"Understandably." Paul pulled down the covers of the bed and puffed the pillows. "We're taught not to do something, and warned about Hell if we do. Then we get married and all of a sudden, we're allowed to be intimate—to be aroused and enjoy each other." He kissed her neck, her cheeks, and her mouth.

Miranda felt electricity and returned the kisses. "I've seen farm animals in tandem, but I don't know how humans mate."

"The trouble with animals is that they're animalistic. Humans should be more loving. I love you. You love me, so don't worry. I've heard that married couples are sometimes awkward at first, but God helps them overcome it."

"Please don't," Miranda said as Paul tried to take her nightgown over her head.

"I won't if nudity makes you too uncomfortable," Paul said, "But remember Adam and Eve? They weren't ashamed of their bodies until after they had sinned."

Miranda relaxed and allowed Paul to remove the gown and touch her. After a while, she returned his touches.

Miranda awoke before dawn feeling blessed. She looked at her handsome husband asleep under the sheet. Since a pitcher of water and a wash bowl were the kitchen, she avoided the pitcher and wash bowl in the bedroom, so she would not wake Paul. After washing and dressing, she lit a lantern and walked outside the hen house for egg collection. The hens voiced cries of fear, but Miranda soothed them with her words. "Hello Girls, I won't hurt you. You'll get to know me soon." She looked for snakes before she put in her hand to pick up eggs.

Outside the hen house, the two donkeys came up to the barbed wire fence to greet Miranda. She petted their faces. “Hello Maisie and Monte. Looks like you did a good job at guarding the cattle and hens last night. The calves are with their mamas. Do you eat what the cattle eat, or do I need to find some special donkey food in the barn?”

“Good morning, Mrs. McCart,” Paul said. “Why don’t you go inside and have some coffee and bacon. I’ll feed the cattle, horses, and donkeys.” He kissed her.

“Aren’t you having breakfast with me?”

“Not this morning, but we will have plenty of meals together.”

Miranda turned down the lantern as the sun rose in the east. She looked into the basket of eggs. “I can bake a pound cake with these eggs.”

“Sounds delicious,” Paul said as he

entered the barn.

"You have a visitor this morning," Mr. Nilsen said as he poured cups of coffee for Mrs. Speer and Miranda. He then went outside.

Mrs. Speer stood up. "Good morning, Mrs. McCart," she said. "I keep hearing wonderful things about you from Esther and Addie. Esther tells me how you and Paul found a dentist and a smith to help her with her teeth."

Miranda smiled. "We only did what the Lord wanted us to do."

Mrs. Speer poured cream in her coffee. "If everyone listened to the Lord and did what He asked, this world wouldn't have its addictions or crime. People would know joy." She paused. "I do what I can to help fallen women. So many of them were led astray when they were destitute and hungry." Mrs. Speer looked Miranda in the eyes. "Esther and Addie want you to attend their healing session tonight."

"I'll have to ask my husband," Miranda said. "But I very much want to attend. If it's dark, he'll have to drive me in the buggy."

"I'm sure Mr. McCart will agree. Any men folk that come with the women get to sit with Mr. Speer at the room on the other side of the dog trot. He's quite a storyteller!"

A Hot Kitchen

Mrs. Speer held up a rounded stick with a cross carved into it. "This is a talking stick. It's another Indian tradition. When the stick is handed to you, you may either share something or simply bless the others. Right now, Addie has the talking stick. She didn't get to talk last time."

Miranda's Exit

episode 32

Cate Murray

A HOT KITCHEN

Miranda and Paul rode the donkeys to the Speer homestead about three miles away. As Paul explained, "Donkeys have good night vision, and these two are familiar with the path between our homestead and the Speer's." Maisie and Monte hesitated when an opossum ran across the road, but the short trip was otherwise smooth. Above, an owl hooted.

Paul introduced his bride to Mr. Speer, and the elderly man greeted her. "Welcome, my dear. Step up to the dog trot. I wanted to come to the wedding, but I had work to do. The ladies meet in the hot room with the stove, and us men folk get the cooler bedroom." Mr. Speer knocked on the kitchen door, and Mrs. Speer opened it.

"Come in! Come in," Mrs. Speer said. In the dim light, Miranda could see Esther, Addie, and two other women sitting around the kitchen table. Esther and Addie hugged her. Esther handed Miranda a hand fan.

“I apologize for the heat,” Mrs. Speer continued, “But you couldn’t expect the men to take the kitchen room, could you?”

“No Ma’am.” Miranda smiled.

“Have you eaten?” Mrs. Speer stood up.

“Yes, we have. Thank you.

“At least have some of my molasses candy.” Mrs. Speer opened a jar sitting in the middle of the table and passed the pieces around. “You know Esther and Addie, but have you met Betty and Caroline?”

“I’m pleased to meet you.” Miranda shook hands with the two women.

Miranda sat down and fanned herself. She put a piece of candy in her mouth. “This is delicious!”

“Yes, it’s my own recipe.” Mrs. Speer placed glasses of water in front of everyone.

"I wish I could try a molasses candy," Esther said, "But after Doc Holliday operated on my teeth, I don't dare. Too sticky."

"Let me explain some things to Miranda," Mrs. Speer told the others. "This is a healing circle. We learn from each other by listening to and accepting each other. We are not here to offer advice unless the other person agrees to accept it. When people have troubles, they often keep them inside, and sometimes they try to forget about them. That's when troubles can fester like a sore. Let's not let this happen. Also, this hot room is somewhat like an Indian sweat lodge." She looked at Miranda. "Have you ever heard of an Indian sweat lodge?"

"No, Ma'am."

"Indians of the Northwest get together in a tipi or a cave, light a fire, meditate, and perspire as a means of purification. If they do without food or water for a while, they sometimes have visions. We don't fast here. In this hot room, you especially need water. But since we only have a hot meeting room, perhaps some perspiration is good for us." Mrs. Speer held up a rounded stick with a cross carved into it. "This is a talking stick. It's another Indian tradition. When the stick is handed to you, you may either share something or simply bless the others. Right now, Addie has the talking stick. She didn't get to talk last time."

Addie took the stick. She first looked down in thought, then made eye contact with the others. "God bless all of you. You've helped me realize that my life's not over. Miranda knew me as a whore, but she never treated me like one. I'm so happy to have her as a guest tonight because she was one of the people whose kindness helped me heal. She is a true Christian. Before, I was so ashamed of selling myself, I'd get budgy on hooch just to make it to my next john." She paused and said, "I still crave a drink sometimes. Usually, I say a prayer and the urge goes away." Addie wiped away some tears and passed the stick to Betty.

Betty smiled and looked at Miranda. "I am from Waco. My mother's family lived there for a century. They were Hueco Indians. When I worked at a bakery there, the pay was low, but I received plenty of leftover pies and cakes. At first, the indulgence was wonderful, but later

I became sick and lost two teeth from excess sugar. When I moved to Bosque County, and heard about Mrs. Speer's healing circle, I stayed away at first. Mrs. Speer is a Cherokee Indian, and I despised the Cherokees. My grandparents had told me about Cherokees raiding their village over 40 years ago. Part of healing includes forgiving."

Outside the open window, Paul's voice was heard. "Hate to interrupt you ladies, but Miranda and I need to get home before it gets too terribly dark!"

Riding away on their donkeys, Miranda asked, "Did you enjoy visiting with Mr. Speer?"

"Yes, he's an engaging old feller. "Did you know that he helped rescue Sam Houston during the Battle of San Jacinto?"

Miranda thought she'd learned many things today.

Miranda's Exile

episode 33

Birthday Surprises

"I read Scientific American magazine." Mr. Nilsen handed her a cup. "They recently published an article about gas engines. Many men overseas are working with such engines. It might not be long before you and I can travel without horses. Someday, we may travel without trains because personal gas engines may move faster."

Miranda put away the cups. "Amazing! In a newspaper, I read about Alexander Graham Bell and the telephone. Do you think ordinary people will ever have them?"

"Quite possibly. People like to talk." Mr. Nilsen and Miranda both laughed.

Cate Murray

BIRTHDAY SURPRISES

Miranda awoke the next day to a widely smiling husband and the smell of coffee. "Happy birthday!" Paul kissed her.

"Thank you. I'll get dressed and fix breakfast."

"Not on your birthday. Mr. Nilsen made a pound cake while we were gone last night. Let's all have a decadent breakfast of birthday cake."

"I thought I smelled something wonderful when we came in!"

Paul left the bedroom and she got dressed.

As Miranda entered the kitchen, Paul and Mr. Nilsen sang together, "For She's a Jolly Good Lady" changing the words from "For He's a Jolly

Good Fellow."

Paul handed her a pair of crocheted gloves. "Maddie made these. She and Esther have quite a business going for them. And Mrs. Nichols bought you this next gift made by Esther." Paul handed Miranda a crocheted cream-colored collar.

"They are both so beautiful! I'll need to sew a dress to go with both of them." Miranda hugged her husband and took her new gifts back to her bedroom.

When she returned, the coffee cup and the cake serving were already on the table. "Mr. Nilsen, thank you so much for the birthday cake. Tomorrow morning, I'll wake up earlier, and milk the cows."

"You are as welcome as you can be, Miranda." Mr. Nilsen laughed. "I'm down to one milk cow now. She's so used to me, she might kick the bucket if anyone else tried to milk her. I named her Old Betsy, the same name as Davy Crockett's rifle. She's a jersey who gives rich milk, and she's really not old despite her name."

"Let's all offer blessings and eat cake," Paul said.

Miranda thanked the Lord for her life, for her home, and for her dear friend, Mr. Nilsen.

After breakfast, Paul went to feed the animals, and Mr. Nilsen insisted on washing the dishes, although he allowed Miranda to dry them. "What do you think life will be like 10 years from now?" she asked her elderly friend.

"I read *Scientific American* magazine." Mr. Nilsen handed her a cup. "They recently published an article about gas engines. Many men overseas are working with such engines. It might not be long before you and I can travel without horses. Someday, we may travel without trains because personal gas engines may move faster."

Miranda put away the cups. "Amazing! In a newspaper, I read about Alexander Graham Bell and the telephone. Do you think ordinary people will ever have them?"

"Quite possibly. People like to talk." Mr. Nilsen and Miranda both laughed.

Paul re-entered the kitchen, overhearing the end of their conversation. “We don’t have a telephone, but we just received a telegram. Those two words have the same root.”

“Is the telegram from your brother in Pennsylvania?” Miranda asked.

“It sure is. Our son will be arriving in Dallas three days from now, so we need to get ready for him. But the telegram does not reveal the boy’s name or his age. He’ll be arriving with a Negro woman, so he’ll be riding in the Negro section.”

“It’s good that your brother provides a caretaker.” Miranda said.

Paul winced. “He refers to her as the mammy. I haven’t heard that word since before the war.”

“The appellation sounds disrespectful nowadays.” Miranda dried her hands on a towel.

“Unfortunately, my oldest sibling has never respected others. If he respected his own flesh and blood, he would have told us the boy's name and age. How old do you guess he may be?"

"For some reason, I imagine him as a four-year-old with blond hair."

"Oddly, I also envision him as about four. Since I, his uncle, had blond hair as a child, possibly this lad also has light hair."

Miranda put her arms around her husband. "I am getting excited about motherhood. Perhaps I need to telegram Clotilda so that she can meet us at the station."

Paul kissed his wife. "We can afford some help. If you infer that the lady caretaker is good with the child, and she needs a job, hire her. We can pay her room, board, and a decent wage."

"Aren't you coming with me?" Miranda asked.

Paul looked at Mr. Nilsen. "If you can take her in the coach, I can keep the ranch running."

"I'll be happy to escort Miranda and meet

the new boy," the elderly man said.

Miranda's heart quickened in her chest. *This will be the first time we'll be apart since we've been married. I'm capable of traveling without him, but I will miss his presence.*

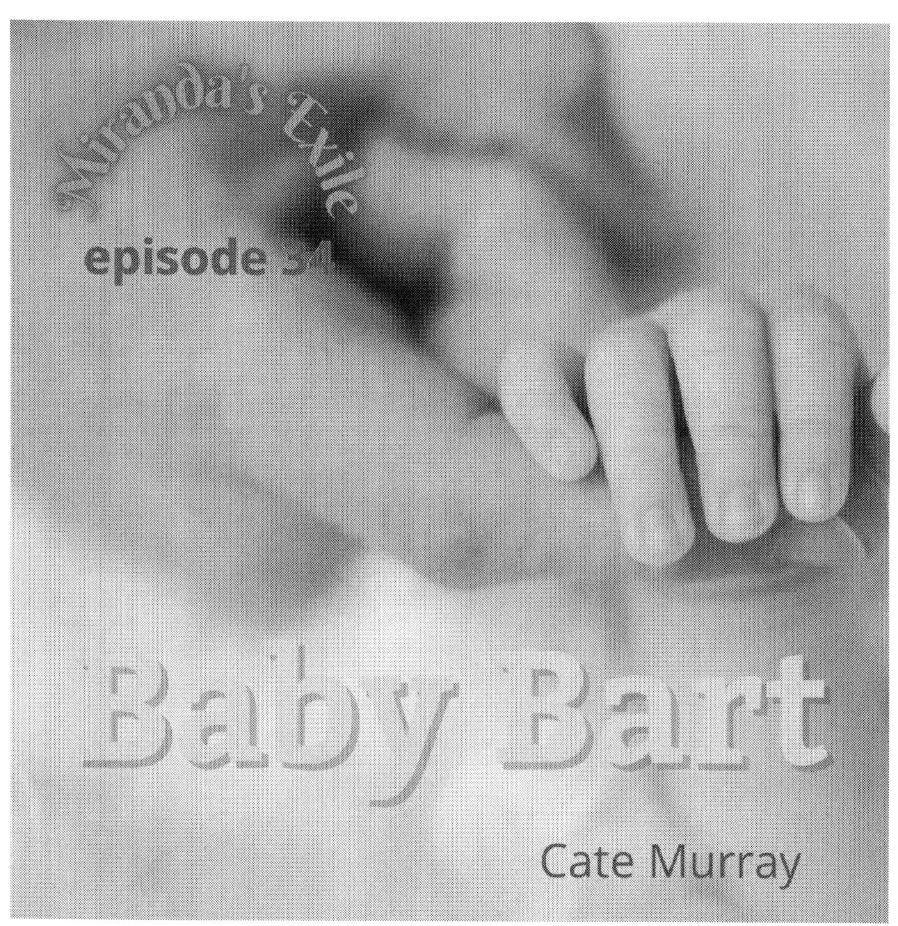
Miranda's Exile
episode 34
Baby Bart
Cate Murray

BABY BART

Miranda, Clotilda, and Mr. Nilsen stood on the platform of the Dallas depot waiting for the child. Clotilda had ridden the streetcar to the train station and met her sister there. Passengers from the latest train crossed the trio on both sides.

"Apparently the travelers on the Negro train exit last," Miranda said. *Why is life so unfair for them?*

Mr. Nilsen spoke, "We've been standing so long, so let's sit down at this bench?"

"That's a great idea," Clotilda remarked, "It's in the shade too." They sat down, and Clotilda continued, "How's married life, Miranda?"

"I am blessed with Paul and with a wonderful friend, Mr. Nilsen. They treated me to a birthday cake and presents three days ago."

"How wonderful! Let me treat you to some gifts before we go home today. Knowing you, you'll choose some toys for your new son."

"That would be lovely. Right now, I don't know his name or his age. Mr. Nilsen has sets of toys that he made for his own sons."

"You are a wonderful friend to my sister," Clotilda said.

"Miranda is like a daughter to me," Mr. Nilsen answered.

A brown-skinned woman carrying a white baby and a bag looked at Miranda and Clotilda. "Good day. One of you Mrs. McCart?"

"I am she." Miranda said.

"I am Yolanda Hutchins," the lady said. "And this young child is Bartholomew McCart. He goes by Bart."

Bart reached out for Miranda, and she took him. "So nice to meet you, Yolanda. And how old is Bart?"

"Mighty fine to know your acquaintance,

Mrs. McCart. He's seven months. I'm afraid Bart is wearing his last diaper. He's going to need another one soon. I admit I threw the dirty ones away. There was no place to wash them on the train."

"Only seven months! Don't worry a bit, Yolanda," Clotilda said. "Let's go to a general store for new diapers, and then we can go to Sanger Brothers, and I'll treat Bart to baby clothes."

Bart began to giggle as Miranda stood up with him. "You've obviously taken good care of Bart, Yolanda. Do you need a job?"

"Yes, Ma'am. I'm going to look around Dallas for work."

As they walked toward the coach, Miranda said, "How about helping me take care of Bart at the ranch?"

Yolanda's eyes lit up. "Mrs. McCart, I would love to come with you! I was getting sad at the idea of leaving Bart. You see, I've been nursing him. The Philadelphia Mrs. McCart was feeding him goat's milk. She had to milk the goat herself until she found me."

“What about your own baby?” Clotilda asked.

Yolanda looked down. “My baby and my husband took sick and died most of a year ago. I’ve been nursing other people’s babies since. Bart’s the only one who isn’t weaned.”

As the group reached the coach, Miranda said, “I am terribly sorry for your loss. You are more than welcome to join us in Bosque County. The only trouble is that it’s over 60 miles southwest of here. We begin the long journey tomorrow.”

“Thank the Lord!” Yolanda said. “I’m blessed to keep loving Bart, and to have a steady job at the same time.

Clotilda sat next to Mr. Nilsen so that she could direct him to the general store. Miranda and Yolanda rode in the coach, and Yolanda nursed Bart.

Miranda looked lovingly at her new son. “Mr. McCart and I both imagined a boy of about four.”

"He's very healthy. Already had measles and mumps. Recovered completely from them both." Yolanda paused, then continued, "He took to squalling for the first part of the train journey. Then he settled down. Bart's quite a good baby."

Miranda said a silent prayer thanking God for the gift of her husband and son.

The foursome and the baby came to Clotilda's home that evening bearing three dozen diapers and three different sizes of baby clothes, enough for Bart to grow into. Carl met the group in the parlor, and Clotilda introduced them.

Carl looked at Yolanda and frowned. "She'll have to stay tonight at Naomi's."

Disturbance in the Nursery

Bart took a wooden horse and put the head in his mouth. “Uhhh! Uhhh!” cried Andrew in protest. Miranda took the horse and handed it to Andrew. Bart began to cry, and Miranda handed him a wooden star. Keeping an eye on the boys, she walked over to a piano and played “Sing a Song of Sixpence.”

Miranda's Exile

episode 35

Cate Murray

DISTURBANCE IN THE NURSERY

Miranda glared at Carl. He glanced at her and turned his gaze to his wife. Clotilda picked up Bart and led Yolanda to the kitchen to introduce the two servants to each other. Miranda followed.

When they reached the kitchen, Miranda told Yolanda, "I'm sorry how my brother-in-law treated you. You'll be better treated at the McCart home in Bosque County."

"Thank you for your kindness, Mrs. McCart," Yolanda said. "I'm used to prejudice."

How can someone ever become accustomed to being treated badly? Miranda wondered.

"Naomi, I want you to meet Yolanda," Clotilda said. "Mr. Graham wants Yolanda to stay with you tonight."

"That'll be fine." Naomi wiped her hands on a towel. "Since my son took a job in Houston, I've had an extra bed."

"Thank you so much, Naomi," Miranda and Yolanda said at the same time. They looked at each other and laughed.

Clotilda showed the baby to Naomi. "This is Bart. Miranda and her husband plan to adopt him."

"What a beautiful baby!" Naomi said.

"I better go change him." Yolanda started to take the baby.

"Don't bother. I'll do it," said Miranda. She took the baby from her sister.

"Andrew should be waking from his nap soon," Clotilda said. "Let's go introduce the two cousins to each other. I'll grab our new purchases, and we'll go upstairs.

In the nursery, Andrew sat up and rubbed

his eyes.

"Andrew, meet your cousin, Bart." Miranda took Bart over to the table to change him. Once Bart was changed, the two boys eyed each other. Miranda and Clotilda placed them in the corner where the toys were kept.

"Bart needs a bath," Clotilda said. "I'll go downstairs and tell Naomi to heat some water."

Bart took a wooden horse and put the head in his mouth. "Uhhh! Uhhh!" cried Andrew in protest. Miranda took the horse and handed it to Andrew. Bart began to cry, and Miranda handed him a wooden star. Keeping an eye on the boys, she walked over to a piano and played "Sing a Song of Sixpence." Bart made happy squeals, and Andrew walked over to his aunt. Bart crawled over and grabbed his mama's foot. In order not to hurt Bart, Miranda decided not to use the pedal. When the song was finished, Miranda said, "I'd sing to you, but I don't like the words." She believed in talking to the young to help them develop language.

Miranda began playing and singing *Frere Jacques*. Bart cooed and Andrew sang toddler-style.

Suddenly, Carl walked in. “Don’t stop playing; it’s beautiful. How about playing a peppy tune like you played in the bawdy house?”

“If you open the door, I’ll play “The Yellow Rose of Texas,” Miranda said.

“Don’t you trust me in a closed room?” Carl laughed. “We’ve got two boys for chaperones. Besides, I’m your brother.”

Miranda stood up from the piano bench and picked up Bart. “You’re my brother-in-law who’s not very respectable. I’m married to Paul McCart, and you’re married to my sister!”

“Put the babies in their bed, and let’s snuggle a little. Babies don’t tell. No one will ever know.” Paul moved closer.

“You get away from me!” Miranda yelled. The boys started screaming.

Mr. Nilsen suddenly burst in. “I heard what you said to Miranda. Now leave her alone.”

"Now come on, old grandpa, let me woo this lovely girl," Carl mockingly pleaded.

"You leave this room right now!" Mr. Nilsen raised his fists. "This lovely girl is an honored married lady. She's like my own daughter."

Clotilda walked in. "What's all this commotion in here?"

"It's just a political argument, Sweetheart," her husband said. "Sometimes I bother my guests with politics!"

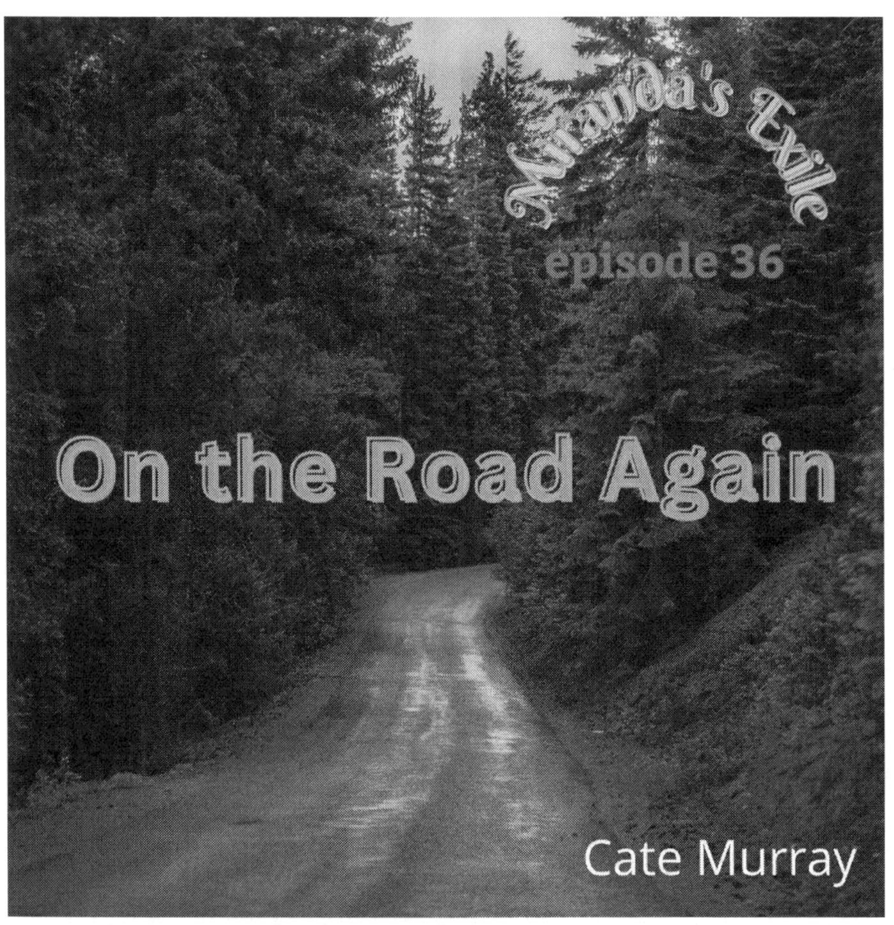
Miranda's Exile
episode 36
On the Road Again
Cate Murray

ON THE ROAD AGAIN

Miranda knew Clotilda had overheard the words in the hall. Yet, Clotilda chose silence rather than confrontation. She looked at Miranda and said, "Let's bathe Bart before supper."

Miranda grabbed an extra diaper and a new baby shirt, and Clotilda found an outfit for Andrew. The two sisters carried the boys downstairs. Andrew and Bart suddenly stopped crying at the same time although Miranda felt tears welling in her own eyes.

Naomi sensed the tension when the women reached the kitchen. "Anything wrong, Mrs. Graham?"

"Not a thing," Clotilda answered. "We just need to bathe the baby." She rolled up a sleeve and placed her elbow in the water in order to judge its temperature. Miranda undressed Bart, and Clotilda sat her son in his high chair.

"Always remember that a baby is very slippery when wet," Clotilda reminded her sister. While Bart was bathed, Naomi fed Andrew.

"Bart can eat tiny bits of food," Yolanda told Miranda. "All right if I feed him?"

"Certainly," the new mother answered.

The roast beef and vegetables tasted delicious, but supper was solemn. Clotilda smiled only when Mr. Nilsen and Miranda spoke of the rolling hills, live oaks, and wildflowers of Bosque County.

"You are always welcome at our ranch," Miranda told her sister. She ignored her brother-in-law, who kept quiet the entire meal and then went to his office.

When bed time came, Miranda was delighted that Clotilda joined her in the bedroom. A petite bed, that had belonged to a younger Andrew, had been placed in the room.

#

At the crack of dawn, Miranda was packed and ready. Mr. Nilsen had awoken even earlier to hitch the horses to the coach. As they were preparing to leave, Yolanda arrived with Naomi. Miranda hugged her sister goodbye and took the baskets of roast beef sandwiches and fried chicken from her.

"Mr. Nilsen," Miranda said, "There's a telegraph office on Main Street. "We need to stop there to let Paul know we're on the way."

"Certainly," Mr. Nilsen said. "It won't take long."

Bart began crying as soon as he and Yolanda entered the coach. "He's hungry," Yolanda said, "I better nurse him."

"You have my permission," Miranda joked. "There's plenty of privacy back here."

At the telegraph office stop, Miranda composed a note to Paul letting him know that they had a seven-month-old son named Bart, and she had hired the boy's nurse, Yolanda.

Once again, she told Paul she loved him. She also let Paul know the group was leaving Dallas. Telegrams were stamped with the time and date, so Miranda knew she didn't need to add that information.

When the coach was on the south road, and Bart was fed and settled, Miranda felt a sadness for her sister and her sister's unfortunate marriage. Knowing that feeling sad for Clotilda did not help her, Miranda said a silent prayer for her and reminded herself to constantly pray for Clotilda. She then thanked God for the joy of Paul, Bart, Mr. Nilsen, and Yolanda.

"What beautiful trees," Yolanda remarked.

"They're Texas Live Oaks," Miranda took Bart from Yolanda, and showed him the life outside the window. "Their leaves stay green in winter."

"In Pennsylvania," Yolanda said, "there are Northern Red Oaks and Chestnut Oaks. They have different bark and different leaves."

"I've heard that Red Oak leaves can

actually turn bright red in the fall," Miranda said.

"They surely do." Yolanda started to add to her conversation when another coach passed. It turned around, and a woman waved her handkerchief to get Miranda's attention. Mr. Nilsen stopped his coach by the side of the road.

"Miss Miranda!" the woman said. "How marvelous to see you again!"

"Mrs. Wright! Come inside this coach so we can visit. I want you to meet Yolanda and Bart."

The tension she had felt at her sister's home now drained from her.

Bartholomew Speaks

Miranda's Exile

episode 37

Cate Murray

BARTHOLOMEW SPEAKS

"Mrs. Wright is the lady for whom I used to sew dresses," Miranda explained to Mr. Nilsen and Yolanda. "Mr. Nilsen, is it all right if we visit briefly? I realize we need to get back on the road soon."

"I don't mind," Mr. Nilsen said. "How do you do, Mrs. Wright?"

"It's good to know you, Mr. Nilsen." Mr. Nilsen left the cab and climbed back up to the box. "Tell me what happened in April, Miranda," Mrs. Wright continued. "You are too gracious a girl to just disappear."

Miranda looked down. "My stepfather became angered at my makeup. He threw me out. The good news is I found my husband in Fort Worth. Bart is his nephew, but he's our son now."

Mrs. Wright took Bart from Yolanda. She exhaled loudly. "Knowing Abner, he beat you before he threw you out."

Yolanda placed a clean diaper on Mrs. Wright's shoulder so that drooling wouldn't stain her dress.

"He did," Miranda answered, "But let's not dwell on Abner. I'm happy with my husband, Paul, now. We're living on a beautiful ranch in Bosque County. How are you doing?"

"I'm fine, but I miss your sewing. May I have your new address?" Mrs. Wright handed Bart and the diaper back to Yolanda. The two women exchanged mailing addresses.

"Please come visit us," Miranda invited.

"I sure will," Mrs. Wright answered. "I love the peace and quiet of the country. In a few years, Johnson County will be disturbed by railroads."

Mrs. Wright stepped down and returned to

her own coach.

As Mr. Nilsen prompted the horses forward, their coach returned to the road. Bart began crying again. Yolanda pulled a rag doll with long, yarn hair out of her bag, and Bart chewed on its feet. After a while, he dropped the doll. He pointed with his hand at a cow outside the window. "Cow," he said.

Miranda was delighted. "He knows a word!"

"Yes Ma'am!" Yolanda answered. "Pretty soon, he'll be saying Mama and Papa. He ain't said it already cause he hadn't known his mama and papa."

"Do you know anything about his real mother?" Miranda asked.

"All I know, Mrs. McCart, is that she wanted to keep him, but her family wouldn't let her." Yolanda paused, then said, "It must of broke her heart to give him away."

Tears welled in Miranda's eyes as she thought of the mother giving Bart away. *Would she want a letter telling her that Bart is doing well?*

Would she want pictures of him?

The coach slowed down, and Miranda's thoughts changed. She told Yolanda, "I forgot to tell you. We will stop about 12 miles from here so that the horses can be exchanged. The mileage yesterday and the mileage today can be taxing on horses, even Clydesdales."

"I believe it," Yolanda said. "I am so glad the horses get a rest."

Yolanda changed Bart again. *How can she balance herself in the coach while she changes the baby?* Miranda wondered. *Perhaps she learned on the train. I would change Bart myself, but I'm afraid I'd accidentally stick him!*

Despite the bumpy road, Miranda managed a long nap. When Mr. Nilsen pulled into Mr. Deporter's farm, she noticed several buggies. As they neared the house, a crowd of people came outside to greet them. Miranda noticed Paul among them.

"I couldn't wait to meet my son," Paul said. "Eddie's staying at the ranch to make sure nothing goes wrong."

Yolanda handed Bart to Paul. Bart fussed a little, then looked at his new father.

"How are you, Bartholomew? That rhymes!" Paul reached out with his free arm and hugged Miranda.

The crowd laughed.

"Paul, I want you to meet Yolanda.

"Mighty fine to meet you, Yolanda. I hear you saved us from having to buy a nanny goat."

Miranda feared he'd said the wrong thing, but Yolanda chuckled with good humor.

Miranda's Exile
episode 38
Asleep in the Manger

ASLEEP IN THE MANGER

The day after Bart arrived at his new home in Bosque County, he drew an admiring audience, sitting in his high chair at the Sunshine Café in Meridian.

"My son's already a politician!" Paul remarked. "He's not shy at all!"

"Bart's an outgoing baby, but he's not mean enough for politics," joked Mr. Jacob Speer.

Miranda spooned some tiny bits of chicken and dumplings into Bart's mouth. After he swallowed the small mouthful, he grabbed Miranda's hand for more.

"Bart may have been born in Pennsylvania," the proprietor's wife said, "But he's a regular little Southerner now. Look how he goes for chicken and dumplings! Why don't you let me feed him, Mrs. McCart. I don't want your lunch to get cold."

"Thanks. I'll take you up on it." Miranda handed the spoon to the proprietor's wife and began enjoying her own lunch.

"As soon as Bart is full, I'll serve you some hot biscuits and molasses cookies. They should be ready soon," the proprietor's wife said.

"I can already smell them," Paul remarked.

"Why don't you check the oven?" Mrs. Epsy Speer said. "I've finished my scrumptious lunch, and I look forward to making friends with Bart." She looked down at the baby, then sat next to him. "How do you do, Mr. Bart? I'm going to have to make you some bibs. Babies never have enough bibs." Mrs. Speer gently scraped Bart's mouth with the spoon and fed him. After Bart swallowed, he smiled at his new friend.

"I'm worried about Esther," Mrs. Speer

whispered to Miranda. "She missed the last two meetings. Maddie says she may have left town."

"She needs our prayers," said Miranda.

"Yes, indeed." Mrs. Speer finished feeding Bart. "She said over and over that you saved her life by finding that terrific dentist."

"Paul introduced me to Doc Holliday who fixed Esther's teeth."

"If I were you, I'd keep Paul." Mrs. Speer winked. "But, seriously, let's pray for Esther." Mrs. Speer hugged Miranda.

After Miranda and Paul finished lunch, he held Bart, then they took a walk around Meridian. "I hope Esther's not back on drugs," Paul whispered.

"I greatly fear that she is. Why else would she quit meetings?" Miranda fanned Bart as they walked past the new rock buildings. After a while, they stopped at a shady picnic table and said a prayer for their troubled friend.

When Miranda and Paul returned home, Yolanda surprised them with scoured floors and a plentitude of food they could heat for supper.

"Thank you," Miranda said, "But you should have let me know you planned to do this much work. I would have stayed home and helped you."

"Mrs. McCart, that's fine. I'm used to hard work. And with a baby crawling around, he needs an extra clean floor."

"You are absolutely right. I should have thought of that," Miranda said.

"No worries," said Yolanda. "He's your first baby."

Paul placed the sleeping Bart into what had been a hay manger. Mr. Nilsen had rigged it with an extra board to protect the active Bart. Paul had remarked the evening before "He'll have to sleep like Jesus did until I finish his crib,"

"I want both of you to sit out on the

porch," Paul said to Miranda and Yolanda. "You need to rest after that long trip."

"That's a great idea, Paul," Miranda said, "Texas sure gets hot in August." She handed one of her fans to Yolanda.

Facing east, away from the sun, Miranda and Yolanda both fell asleep in their rockers. They awoke at about the same time, and Yolanda said, "I better check on the baby. He might need changing."

"Thanks. Bring him out here when you're finished." Miranda wiped the perspiration from her face with the handkerchief.

Suddenly, she heard Yolanda's distressed voice, "The baby's gone! Could he have fallen out the window?"

Miranda ran around to the side where the open window was next to Bart's temporary bed. The petunia bushes were disturbed by two adult footprints.

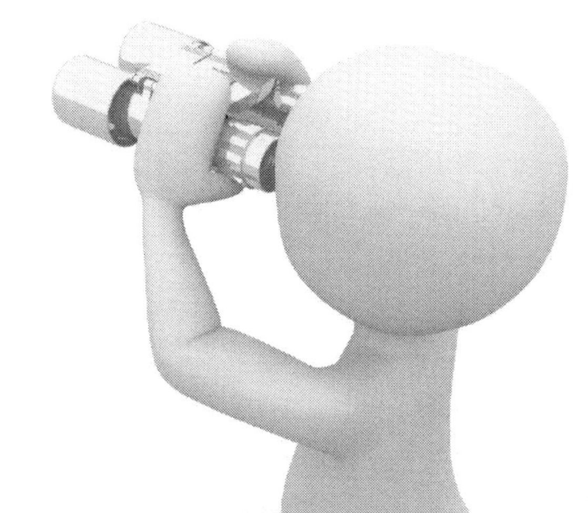

Search Party

Miranda's Exile

episode 39

SEARCH PARTY

Miranda heard herself wailing. She then felt Paul's hands on her shoulders. He said, "You stay here. I'll get the sheriff. We'll find Bart." He quickly left.

Yolanda's voice said, "I'll stay with you, Mrs. McCart. Let me fix you some tea."

Miranda lifted her head and wiped away her tears. "Why didn't we wake up when Bart was taken?"

"Someone quiet took him. Maybe they'll take good care of him," Yolanda answered. "Lonely people sometimes snatch babies. They feel like they deserve them. Ain't right."

Yolanda went into the kitchen to boil water for the tea. When she returned, Miranda asked, "Do you suppose Bart's mother came and got him?"

Yolanda looked up in thought. “If she did, it’d be awful spooky. She’d have to follow us here. I once adopted a little kitten, and the mama came and grabbed him. I ended up taking care of both of them. Fed the mama cream so she’d stay.”

When the tea was ready, Miranda and Yolanda both sat and sipped. Miranda looked at her new friend. “I’m so glad you’re here, Yolanda.” She burst out in tears again. “Will you stay with us no matter what?”

Yolanda wrapped her arms around Miranda. “I wouldn’t think of leaving you and Mr. McCart. As long as you need me, I am here. I have faith that baby’s going to be found. Let’s pray together.”

Not long after Miranda and Yolanda finished praying, the house buzzed with women. “Try not to worry,” Mrs. Nichols said. “Your husband, the sheriff, and Eddie have all gone searching for Bart.”

“Thank you for letting me know, Mrs. Nichols,” Miranda answered.

"He must have been taken by Indians," a woman said. "They're fascinated by little blonde haired, blue eyed babies."

"Nonsense! Mrs. Brown," Mrs. Espsy Speer said. "The last Indians to leave this area were Tonkawas. They are very gentle. They've never kidnapped children."

"What about the Comanches? They kidnap children!" Mrs. Brown continued.

"The last Comanches in this area, and they might have been another tribe, were spotted by Eddie six or seven years ago," Mrs. Nichols said. "They caused no trouble."

Mrs. Brown was adamant. "Maybe it was a coyote or a wolf!"

"They come out at night," Mrs. Speer said.

"If they're hungry, and they sense food, they'll appear in the day. I've seen them!"

"Mrs. Brown," Miranda said. "We have two

donkeys who guard against coyotes and wolves. And besides, two shoe prints were found right by the baby's window."

"Mrs. Brown," Mrs. Nichols interjected. "Can't you see your suggestions are unsettling to Mrs. McCart? She just received this baby, and now someone has taken him!"

"I know you're just trying to help, Mrs. Brown." To the others, Miranda said, "Yolanda and I were speculating that Bart's real mother may have followed us and taken him."

"You're his real mother now," Mrs. Nichols said.

"Yes, I am," Miranda agreed, "But imagine what it would be like to give birth to a baby, then have others take him from you."

"Was she married?" Mrs. Brown asked.

"I don't know," Miranda answered. "But whether she was or she wasn't, it would be horrific to have to surrender a child."

“Excruciating,” Mrs. Speer agreed.

The group heard a knock at the door. Yolanda answered, and Eddie, Mr. Jacob Speer, and a young Mexican boy entered the house.

“Ladies,” Eddie said. “This is Pablo. He may have spotted your baby, Mrs. McCart.”

Miranda looked at Pablo, and he looked at her. “A woman. Silver teeth. Pablo pointed to his incisors.”

“Thank you, Pablo!” Miranda looked at Mrs. Speer.

“*Esther!*” they both said at the same time.

God Bless Us
Miranda's Exile
Final Episode!

GOD BLESS US

"Under a tree, they were," Pablo explained.

"Sit down, Pablo," Miranda said. "Would you like some tea?"

"Yes, Ma'am."

Miranda served Pablo. "Can you tell me the direction of the tree from here?"

Pablo pointed. "East. Not far from Steele's Creek."

How I want him to take me to Bart and Esther, but I need to wait for Paul and Sheriff Careton. No, Bart needs rescue as soon as possible.

"Pablo, please take me to my baby. I'll warm your tea when we return."

"Yes, Ma'am."

"No, wait here, Mrs. McCart," Mrs. Brown said. "Wait for the men. A doped up woman is bound to be dangerous!"

"I'll go with you," Mrs. Speer said. "Esther will listen to me."

"I'll go too," Yolanda said. "Bart will be hungry."

"Esther should be hungry too." Miranda grabbed a sandwich that someone had made, and the foursome left.

After the group had walked about a quarter of a mile, Miranda heard Paul's voice, "Where are you going? I told you to stay home!"

Miranda turned around. She saw Paul and the sheriff on horseback. "Pablo found Bart with Esther! He's going to show me where they are."

"Hello Pablo," Paul said. "Why don't you mount my horse and show the sheriff where you saw the baby. I'll take the ladies home."

"Can one of you carry a baby on a horse?" Miranda asked.

"I can. Don't worry," Sheriff Careton answered.

As Miranda, Paul, Mrs. Speer, and Yolanda walked toward the house, Paul explained, "Pablo used to scout for us on trail rides. He has great intuition, and he knows Indian sign language."

"God bless Pablo. He found our baby." Miranda paused, then said, "I'm really sorry about leaving the house. I didn't know if Bart was in distress."

Paul placed his arm around his wife. "I understand. But we don't know what type of condition Esther is in. The sheriff is good at calming intoxicated people. Let's let him handle it."

#

When Sheriff Careton and Pablo returned with Bart and a contrite Esther, Miranda immediately embraced her crying child. He was wearing an ineffective burlap diaper, so

Miranda's dress became soiled.

"I'll clean him up and nurse him, so you can get changed," Yolanda said. Miranda cried with joy as she walked to her bedroom to change.

When Miranda returned, Sheriff Careton said, "I arrested Esther, and I'm going to jail her."

Miranda handed Esther the sandwich she was going to bring to her. "Why did you take our baby?"

"I'm so sorry." Esther broke out in tears. Her face was already red and tear-streaked. "I can't have a baby. I thought you could have many." She looked down. "Before I came to Mrs. Porter's, I had an abortion. Nearly bled to death. I'm so sorry."

"Thank you for being truthful," Miranda said. "Thank you for not hurting Bart."

"I would never have hurt him!" Esther insisted.

As the sheriff escorted his prisoner toward the door, Mrs. Speer said, "I'll come see you and bring cookies. When you're released, you may come live in the cabin again. And attend meetings."

"I can come back to the meetings?"

"Yes," Mrs. Speer answered. "You've fallen away from the healings. But it's just like falling off a horse. You get back on as soon as you can."

Miranda remembered her own exile by her stepfather, and all that she'd been through. So much had changed, and things now were better.

As soon as the company left, Yolanda had finished nursing Bart. "He's all right but tired. He'd only take a few mouthfuls." She rocked the baby in his room.

Paul led the invocation of thanksgiving. "Let's all thank the Lord who guarded our baby." Before the grateful prayer was finished, a knock was heard at the door.

"Are you Mr. McCart? Where do you want us to place the piano?"

"A piano?" Miranda asked.

Paul smiled and winked at his wife. To the two men, he said, "Bring it inside, and I'll let the lady of the house decide where she wants it."

Miranda kissed Paul then guided the men to the parlor and indicated where the piano should reside.

She walked back to Paul and smiled up at him.

"I have a feeling things should be going our way from now on."

He pulled her into his arms and kissed her.

"Honey, I believe your feelings are about right."

– The End

ABOUT THE AUTHOR

Cate Murray

Catherine Murray teaches at a community college in Texas. She studied creative writing under Caroline Gordon at the University of Dallas. She holds a Ph.D from Texas Woman's University.

PRAISE FOR AUTHOR

Praise From Author C. L. Nichols - Amazon Customer
5.0 out of 5 stars

Hidden Candle is Inspiring & Suspenseful!

After a tragic beginning, the heroine becomes a nurse who falls in love with a man from the Underground.

- C. L. NICHOLS - AMAZON CUSTOMER

OUTSKIRTS OF THE WOODS
5.0 out of 5 stars
Get this for the poetry!!!
Cate wields similes like warriors wield scimitars. There is so much in these pieces that touch the soul. It's gold.

-JULIE

BOOKS BY THIS AUTHOR

Josephine's Journey

In 1960, Texas Josephine McKelvey marries folk singer Jonathan. She moves to San Francisco with him and begins her new adventures and misadventures, encountering Jack Kerouac, Allen Ginsberg, Dr. David Smith, and Charles Manson.

Josephine delivers a beautiful baby and enters U. C. Berkeley. She joins the Free Speech movement and learns that free speech is not the goal of its organizers. With the help of two wise women who have escaped prisons in the Soviet Union and Cuba, and another lady who was deceived by her civil rights group, Josephine discovers many social justice organizations have corrupt roots.

Josephine & Jon convert to Catholicism, but Jonathan ventures away to sit at the feet of a famous Indian guru.

The journey ends in 1969.

Outskirts Of The Woods

Outskirts of the Woods Has your paradigm ever shifted? This collection illustrates the changes of a spiritual seeker: Vedantic to Christian, Pro-Choice to Pro-Life, and Bohemian to Settled.

BERTHA'S BUTTER CLUB, a one-act comedy, jabs at every person who thinks they have the formula to make others lose weight.

DYSLEXIC chronicles my many and long attempts to seek a cure.

Other essays compare convicted murderers Susan Atkins and Karla Faye Tucker, and uncover the tragic deaths of two abortive women. Also included is an essay based on a Caroline Gordon short story, my creative writing mentor at the University of Dallas.

OUT OF THE MOUTHS OF BABES: This one-act has a 13 year old pro-life debater who greatly loves her dad who performs abortions.

The play is followed by DAUGHTER OF INDIA, a biography of my aunt, Sanskrit scholar Camille Svensson.

At last comes poetry! One poem can hold a whole universe -- finding love, losing love, reaching for God but touching a dark hole and discovering the true God.

This book covers forty years of love, disillusionment, and then finding love again.

Hidden Candles

In Hidden Candle, Annalise Kessler loses her infant brother to the Nazi nurse of her village. Germany invades Poland, and World War II begins. Not always does Annalise know whom to trust.

Forbidden Thoughts: In the 1925 Soviet Union, thoughts can subconsciously become words, so lovers Elena and Petr carefully confide solely in each other. They discover messages hidden in a wall from Alexandra, a woman who mysteriously disappeared. Elena and Petr must act quickly to save other innocents.

Mother's Occult Stories -- These stories feature Chia Ellis, a young female Greek professor, who uses her psychic skills to help others heal from their karmic wounds. These wounds are of varied nature.

The play, Intersection, is based on a true crime that took place near the intersection of Highways 77 and 81 in Hillsboro, Texas.

The memoir "Duped and Redeemed" reveals two separate vital life intersections, one chosen and the other unchosen.

Other essays include topics such as dyslexia, Joseph Pearce, and Lee Harvey Oswald.

The short stories are My Name (My Identity), Mother Hilda, and Three Days of Darkness.

Josephine's Journey
Adventures & Misadventures in the 1960s
Cate Murray

Cate Murray

outskirts of the woods

Poems, Plays, Essays
and a Biography

Hidden Candles

Novellas, Stories, Essays, a Memoir & a Play

Cate Murray

Made in the USA
Columbia, SC
25 January 2023